"We'd be lovers," Luke told her

"And will I live here? And be your...
'pillow friend,' as I think your cousin
termed that particular kind of
woman?" Colette questioned coolly.
"Do you usually have your pillow
friends living here?"

"I've never had one living here. You'll
be the first," he added with a smile.

Marveling at the steadiness of her
voice when she was so close to tears,
Colette asked, "Has this Stella ever
been your—"

"If she had," replied Luke slowly,
"there would be no question of her
ever becoming my wife."

"Because Greeks never marry their
mistresses," Colette remembered.

"Greek women understand these
things," he said matter-of-factly.
"Stella might be jealous and give me
the cold shoulder for a while, but
she'd come around once you
and I parted."

ANNE HAMPSON

a rose from lucifer

Harlequin Books

TORONTO • LONDON • LOS ANGELES • AMSTERDAM
SYDNEY • HAMBURG • PARIS • STOCKHOLM • ATHENS • TOKYO

Harlequin Presents edition published February 1982
ISBN 0-373-10483-9

Original hardcover edition published in 1979
by Mills & Boon Limited

CHAPTER ONE

IT was nothing new for Colette to come in from work to find her mother crying. She stood by the kitchen door, a sigh on her lips and a brooding expression in her big, limpid blue eyes. It could not go on, she had decided a long time ago, yet what was the way out of it all? How could she and her mother escape?

'Darling. . . .' She flung down her handbag and went towards her, to where she was standing over the sink, a forlorn figure prematurely aged, her hands red and chapped, ingrained with dirt from the potatoes she was peeling. 'What is it this time, dearest—him again, or Elspeth?' Colette hated them both, father and daughter, and cursed the day her widowed mother had fallen victim to the charms of a man like Lewis Whitney.

'It's Elspeth—Lewis isn't in yet.' A sob escaped her as she turned, fluttering a hand to remove the wisps of dry and greying hair from her forehead. 'She's been in here, complaining that her bedroom hasn't been dusted today, but I've felt so ill——'

'Ill?' broke in Colette anxiously. 'What's wrong, Mother?'

'Nothing serious,' Mrs Whitney hastened to assure her. 'A headache, love, and my back——' She straightened automatically and put a damp hand behind her, pressing it against the knot that tied her apron. 'I could do with a rest—a holiday. But there isn't a chance, and even if there was I'd only have to come back to this drudgery.'

Colette put an arm about her waist and kissed her tenderly on the cheek.

'Come and sit down, pet, and I'll make you a cup of tea.' She led her through the door, to the living-room and then to the sofa. 'Where's Elspeth now?' she wanted to know, a dangerous sparkle in her eyes.

'In her room, getting ready to go out with that awful foreigner she's taken up with. I hate him coming here, and I know you do as well.' Mrs Whitney sat down, wiping her hands down her apron. Colette turned away to the kitchen, her mind switching for a moment to the foreigner of whom her mother had spoken. Luke Marlis, whose first encounter with Colette had had an unbelievable effect on her, setting her pulses racing and her heartbeats speeding overrate. Elspeth had met him at the Hunt Ball; he had obviously fallen for her in a big way because ever since then he had taken her out every night, and for the last two week-ends they had gone away, to stay in a country hotel somewhere in Surrey. Tall and dark, with eyes that seemed to be black, and which always had a look of arrogance in their depths, Luke Marlis was the most formidable man Colette had ever met ... but he was also the most attractive. ...

Thrusting out his image, she went to the tap and filled the kettle. Should she go up and tackle her step-sister? She frowned and decided against an encounter where, if past experience was anything to go by, she would be sure to come off worst. Elspeth with her superior education, her innate poise and air of superiority, to say nothing of her cutting tongue, had from the first been able to make Colette feel small and inferior. Then there was the difference in their ages, Colette being a mere seventeen while Elspeth was almost twenty-five, a woman of the world who made no secret of her past affairs, nor of the fact that she intended using her looks to capture a millionaire.

'And if he has a title so much the better,' she had said, deliberately fixing her eyes on Colette's disfiguring birthmark which ran from one side of her nose, right across her left cheek, and down to the curve of her throat. 'You'll never get anyone at all,' she had added cruelly, then amended this by saying that it was just possible that Colette would manage to get one of the local farm labourers to offer her marriage, and if so, she ought to seize the opportunity without hesitation.

'Here's your tea, darling.' Colette had laid a tray with dainty porcelain from the cabinet in the hall, and she had used the beautiful silver from the canteen. Mrs Whitney frowned, but before she could speak Colette said,

'You've a right to use the best things. Why should they be just for show?'

'Because,' snarled a voice from the open doorway which led to the hall and stairs, 'those things happened to belong to my mother!' Elspeth, superb in a trouser suit of light green velvet, her dark hair beautifully gleaming and framing a face of incredible beauty, came into the room with a purposeful stride and stood over Colette, her cheeks fused with angry colour. 'How dare you! And with this woman in such a state—looking like some fishwife——' She glowered at Mrs Whitney. 'Put that down! Don't you dare to drink from that cup!'

All Colette's restraint broke at these insults flung at her mother and without even attempting to control the urge that drove her she picked up the plate on which she had put some biscuits and flung it across the floor. The cup came after it and the saucer followed.

'There!' she cried, her eyes blazing with fury. 'That's

what I think of your precious mother's pots!'

'By God. . . .' Elspeth stared, her big brown eyes fairly bulging in their sockets. 'By God, Colette, you'll suffer for this when my father comes in!'

'Colette dear, you ought not to have let your temper get the better of you.'

'I was goaded, Mother! I won't have her insulting you! I don't care if the set's ruined. I've a good mind to smash the whole lot!'

'You've destroyed the value.' Elspeth's voice was back to normal; she seemed rather dazed now by what had happened.

'She didn't think I had it in me,' was Colette's conviction, spoken to herself.

'All the value's gone,' continued Elspeth, stooping to pick up one or two of the broken pieces of Derby porcelain. 'It's over a hundred and fifty years old, that tea-set, and was worth a fortune.' She turned on Colette, her face resuming its ugly twist. 'You bitch! You malicious little bitch! Because you're so damned ugly you've got a grudge against everyone——!'

'She isn't ugly!' Mrs Whitney had risen from the sofa, and she burst into tears. 'Why do you keep saying such unkind things, Elspeth?'

'She *is* ugly!'

'Oh . . .!' Mrs Whitney's tears flowed even faster, and a deep, deep sigh issued from Colette's lips. 'She is *not*, I tell you! Look at her eyes and her hair——'

'Mother,' interrupted Colette gently, 'I do wish you wouldn't take it so much to heart. It's there, and no one is to blame. It could happen to anyone, and if I don't mind why should you?'

'You do mind,' sneered Elspeth, dropping the broken pieces of porcelain back on to the thick-pile carpet. 'I've seen you looking in the mirror, and wishing you looked like me.'

Colette glanced at her with contempt.

'So you believe I'd like to look like you?' She shook her head. 'No, Elspeth. You might be beautiful, but beauty doesn't hide the hardness of your face.'

The other girl turned away, stared down at the broken crockery for a moment and then went from the room.

'Darling, why did you do it?' cried Mrs Whitney. 'Things are bad enough without your adding to it. What will Lewis say——? Oh, I wish I were dead!'

Colette swallowed the pain in her throat. Her mother had been so thrilled, three years ago, when she had met the impressive and prosperous businessman, Lewis Whitney, and he had become interested in her. She and Colette had been living from hand to mouth since the death of her husband four years previously, and she had at last decided to sell the small terraced house and take a rented flat, because the house was in need of so much repair that she knew it would be impossible to meet the expenses which the repairs would incur. Then out of the blue Lewis had proposed, for at that time Renie Moore was beautiful, and she looked much younger than her thirty-six years.

'It's a miracle!' she had told her fourteen-year-old daughter excitedly. 'He's well-off and has a lovely house in its own grounds—in Fairley, and you know how posh that district is! It'll be wonderful for you, love, to be brought up in luxury, and to meet really *nice* people!'

It had never been wonderful for Colette, nor had she met any of these 'really nice' people her mother had hopefully mentioned. Firstly, she disliked Lewis Whitney on sight, and his daughter had instantly made her feel inferior, a gauche little schoolgirl whose presence in the house would have to be tolerated because there was nowhere else she could go.

'When you're old enough to go out to work,' Elspeth had said, 'you'd better leave here, because neither my father nor I are happy at the idea of having you around indefinitely.' She had always flinched at sight of the disfigurement at first, but as she became used to it she simply took it for granted, but that did not deter her from remarking on it now and then, just to remind Colette that it was there.

It had very soon dawned both on Renie and her daughter that Lewis had merely wanted a housekeeper, someone to run his home cheaply. For he was the meanest man they had ever met and absolutely refused to pay a housekeeper the wages that were being demanded these days. Mrs Whitney had been a drudge almost from the beginning, and what infuriated Colette was that her stepfather had the added convenience of a woman to sleep with. He never bought her mother a present, never remembered their wedding anniversary. Nor did he take her anywhere, and about twelve months ago he had begun going out every single night in the week, returning at well past midnight. Meriel Vincent, a friend of Colette's who worked in the same office as she—both as typists—had seen him out dining with another woman, and she had told Colette about this but, naturally, Colette had kept it to herself.

'It's rumoured that he's always been a philanderer,' Meriel had said frowningly. She was very much attached to Colette, and she also had a warm feeling for her mother. 'What a pity she ever met him. Your mother was so pretty at one time that she could have had anyone.'

Colette had nodded in agreement. She and Meriel had been friends at school; both had been forced to forget all about further education, for both had widowed mothers. They left school together, applied

for the posts which offered free tuition, and attended
the Sight and Sound College in Liverpool where they
did exceedingly well, passing their exams and then
taking up the jobs which they held at present. But it
was not very well paid work; they were only seventeen
and therefore could not expect to be anywhere near to
the maximum salary. This meant frustration for
Colette, because if only she could earn more then she
and her mother could think of leaving the house where
they had found nothing but unhappiness. She had
asked her mother about the money she received for the
terraced house, thinking that there must surely be
enough for them to furnish a flat and with a bit over to
tide them on until Colette was earning more, or until
her mother managed to find work of some kind.

'We could take one of those flats at Saltney,' she had
said eagerly. 'You know, the ones they're building.
They were to be for sale, but now they're to let. Say we
can have one, Mother.'

'I gave your stepfather all the money——'

'Gave it to him?' frowned Colette. 'But it's yours!'

'He wanted to invest it for me—said I'd get nothing
in the ordinary bank. When I asked him recently what
he'd done with it he said the investment had gone sour
—whatever that means—and the whole lot was lost.'

Colette hadn't believed him, but she soon realised
the futility of voicing her suspicions, either to her
mother or to the man who had robbed her. He was a
pinchfist who, having got his greedy hands on the
money, had no intention of parting with one penny of
it.

When Colette had started work in the office Elspeth
had asked her father to tell her to go, and Colette had
wondered what either she or her mother could do if he
acceded to his daughter's wish. However, as Colette

was by this time an asset in the house, always busy helping her mother with the hundred and one chores, he
hesitated about losing her services. His scheming mind
had also taken into consideration the contribution she
could make towards the food bill, and in addition he
had the bright idea of disposing with the services of
the part-time gardener, and handing over his tasks to
Colette. And so she had been allowed to stay, much to
the disgust of her stepsister who, for some inexplicable
reason, seemed at times not only to resent her but to be
jealous of her. This latter impression remained with
Colette in spite of the sneering depredations she was
periodically receiving from the girl whose beauty left
any man she met craving to be more to her than a mere
acquaintance.

She had had many beaux, even before Colette had
met her; she was now head over heels in love with the
dark Greek who, it was rumoured, was a millionaire
twice over. His home was on the delectable island of
Attikon, one of several small islands of the Sporades,
lying to the north of Euboea. He was in England on
business, the nature of which Elspeth—if she knew it—
had kept to herself.

However, Colette was sure that his stay in this
country was coming to an end and she was naturally
curious as to what would transpire between him and
Elspeth in the near future.

'Here's your stepfather!' The frantic exclamation
brought Colette from her reverie and she turned, following the direction of her mother's terrified gaze.

'He can't kill me,' said Colette, but was nevertheless
aware that her knees felt weak and that her heart was
racing. Anger surged at the idea that Lewis could get
her into this nervous state even before he had entered
the house. Who was he to affect her calm like this?—

to upset her nerves! Her mother was in a dreadful state, and in order to make an attempt to steady her, she asked her to assist in gathering up the broken bits of porcelain.

'He'll be furious! Oh, Colette, what made you lose your temper like that? It's not your way at all. You usually manage to ignore that creature's insults.'

'When they're directed at me, yes,' agreed Colette, her eyes grim. 'But when she started on you—well, I just couldn't hold myself in. To the devil with the pair of them! We'll pack up and leave!'

'Don't be silly. Where would we go?'

'He ought to be made to give you back that money.'

'His word would be accepted in a court of law, he once told me when I was being awkward over it. The money was lost in speculation and that's that. I was willing for him to invest it, you see, so I've no come-back.'

'If you leave him,' said Colette thoughtfully, 'he'd have you to keep.'

A thin and faintly contemptuous smile hovered for a second or two on Mrs Whitney's pale lips.

'You know very well, Colette, that he'd wriggle out of anything like that. Why, as it is I never get a penny of my own—nothing for necessities like replacements of underwear or even a coat. What bit I do have for myself comes from you.'

Colette frowned heavily, thinking of the way her stepfather would get down, once a month, to probing into the household expenses. He would want to know where every single penny of the 'petty cash' had gone. With the food bills and all else appertaining to the general expenses, he insisted on paying them himself, by cheque, after receiving—and carefully perusing—the bills of the various traders. In this way he was able to ensure that his wife was unable to touch anything except the small amount he put in a box for incidentals. And as every penny of that had to be accounted for, Mrs Whitney could not even wangle the odd copper for herself. Most of what Colette earned was handed over to Lewis, but he was ignorant of the small rise she had been given, and it was from this that she was able to give her mother a little spending money and also have a little for herself extra from that which Lewis allowed her. Mean as he was with everyone else he was generous with his daughter. Elspeth was allowed to keep all she earned, with the result that she was always superbly dressed, was able to buy costly perfumes and cosmetics, and she was a client of the most exclusive hairdresser in town.

Lewis entered and hard upon his heels came Elspeth who, without even waiting for him to say hello to her, poured out what had happened. Some of the bits of china were still lying around and she pointed to them, her accents choked, her eyes blazing as she said finally,

'Poor Mother's treasured Derby! All these years unharmed by generations of servants, and now—now to be wantonly destroyed by that—that back-street bitch who probably thinks they can be replaced at Woolworths!'

Lewis's eyes, glittering with rising fury, moved with slow deliberation from his daughter's furious countenance to the floor, then to the cowering figure of his wife. Colette, blazing with anger at seeing her mother so terrified, knew why murders were committed. Gentle though she was, she could at this moment have killed the man who had brought her mother to this state of utter degradation. She spoke; she had to, before he could deliver the tirade that was hovering on his tight-lipped, cruel mouth.

'It was Elspeth's fault! She insulted my mother—
said she looked like a fishwife! Where is her respect, I'd
like to know? She didn't consider my mother fit to
drink from those cups—so I showed her what I thought
about them!'

'You smashed them deliberately?' The voice was low
and harsh, the eyes burning with wrath. 'Did you
know their value?'

'I couldn't care less about their value,' she flashed. 'If
they're so damned precious then go and hide them
somewhere! Put them in the bank! I'm sure we don't
want them here!'

'Here?' repeated her stepfather softly, moving with
almost animal stealth towards her. 'Is it possible that
you've forgotten that this is my house you're living in?'

'You've always taken good care that we never forget
it,' she returned contemptuously.

'She wants a thrashing!' blazed Elspeth, goading her
father as she saw his stealthy approach towards the spot
where Colette stood. Too late Colette grasped his intention; she was not quick enough to dodge out of his
way and she cried out in pain as, making a grab at her
arm, he twisted it savagely.

'You brat!' he snarled, crimson colour creeping up
the sides of his mouth. 'I ought to slap your ugly face—
disfigure it on the other side for you!' Instead he flung
her from him and turned to his trembling wife, moving
close to tower over her. 'As for you—you've been told
never to touch anything of value. You've never been
used to such treasures and you aren't capable of hand-
ling them! You'll see that your daughter pays for the
damage——'

'She hasn't that sort of money, Lewis,' cried his wife
desperately. 'You know she hasn't, not when you take
so much from her!'

'Well, I'll be taking more!' He looked her over con-temptuously. 'Go and get yourself washed and changed. I'm sick of you waiting on the table looking as if you haven't washed for months!'

Colette and her mother stared at one another as, having delivered this, Lewis strode from the room, followed by Elspeth, who slammed the door behind her.

'I'm sorry, Mother. All this is my fault.' Colette looked away, her eyes filling up. 'I ought to have held my tongue.'

'And controlled your temper, child. That tea-set was beautiful. I often stood and admired it, wondering what it was worth. And now three pieces are broken——' She stopped, waiting for Colette to look at her again. 'It was nothing less than vandalism, Colette, and you can't really blame Lewis for being angry.'

Colette, whose arm was giving her some considerable pain, spoke impulsively, saying what was in her mind, without even thinking what effect it would have on her mother.

'I wish I could get away! I'd be willing to go as a maid to escape from this misery——' She stopped, appalled, and ran to her mother. 'I'd never leave you, darling. I couldn't!'

Her mother looked at her mistily, her mouth trem-bling.

'As a matter of fact I've been thinking about it, Colette. There's no reason why you should be suffering for my mistake. I feel you should be moving, making your own way in the world. It's struck me that Mrs Vincent wouldn't mind taking you as a boarder—in fact, I rather think she'd welcome you, as you'd be paying your way——'

A lift of Colette's hand stopped her. She need think

no more about it, declared her daughter. There was no
question of their separating, and certainly no question
of her leaving her mother to battle on alone in what
Colette had often referred to as the 'enemy camp'.

'We're in this together. Your marriage could have
benefited me, remember? You expected it to do so. It
hasn't benefited either of us, as things have turned out,
but that's by the way.' She paused, looking at her, remembering how, not so long ago, she had been young
and pretty. A simple person, as was Colette, they had
had little of the real refinements of life, or the benefits
of the so-called 'affluent society' of today. Her father
had never earned much money in his job of delivery
man for a local bakery, but he was respected and
trusted with the firm's money. Theirs was a typical
working-class existence, and Colette as a child had had
all the love she had needed, both from her father and
her mother. The tragedy of losing her husband had left
Mrs Moore drained of emotion and for a while she had
tended to neglect her daughter, but that had soon
passed and during the succeeding years of her widow-
hood she and Colette had drawn very close to one another. It came as a devastating blow to Colette to learn
that her mother was contemplating putting someone
else in her father's place, but at the same time, with a
wisdom far greater than would be expected from a
fourteen-year-old, she had seen it all from her mother's
point of view. She was young; she was having a terribly
hard life, and there was the added anxiety of the repairs
needed to the house. Marriage to Lewis Whitney came
as the panacea for all the troubles assailing Colette's
mother who, carried away also by the attentions of a
man who in her eyes was little less than exalted, agreed
to marry him without having given the matter much
thought at all. Certainly she had not foreseen a life

like this where both she and Colette were constantly at the beck and call, not only of her husband but of his daughter as well.

'Not matter what you say, Colette,' her mother was murmuring, a sob in her voice, 'I feel you ought to make what you can of your own life.' Involuntarily her eyes darted to the disfigurement and she flinched. Colette said gently,

'You're thinking that I shall never marry? Well, that's in the hands of the gods, Mother, and I shan't complain if no one ever wants me——'

'You're so sweet, dearest, never complaining, accepting it without rancour the way you do.' She looked at her tenderly, managing a brief smile. Colette said quietly,

'Troubling myself over it won't do a bit of good, so why waste my time and thoughts on something so unproductive?'

But she often did look in the mirror, just as Elspeth had said, and wonder what she would be like without the scar. As her mother always said, her hair was beautiful—honey-gold and long, shining with health and slightly waved so that the ends turned up in natural half-curls, which rested on her sloping shoulders. Her skin was clear and unblemished except where the scar was, the deep purple scar that had almost broken her mother's heart when she first saw it. Colette's thoughts wandered, to words spoken to her by a nice young man —Davy Maddox—who flattered her, appearing not to have noticed the blemish as he declared that her eyes were like saucers, and the incredible colour of an azure sky in June. He had said she had a kissable mouth, beautifully-contoured features and, lastly, the figure of an angel. Colette had lapped it all up avidly even though the young man himself was by no means her ideal.

Her ideal.... Her eyes brooded, the vision of Luke Marlis intruding, erasing all else.... Luke, whose real name was Lucius, derived from Lucifer, the 'demon flame god' of ancient mythology.

Colette would not allow herself to admit that his attraction was so overpowering that she could have spent all her days thinking about him. He belonged to Elspeth, but even if he hadn't he would never have looked at her. It was laughable even to imagine his doing so ... and yet there were times when Colette did allow her fanciful thoughts free rein, and she was in his arms, his tall strong body pressing to hers, his pagan mouth demanding, taking, possessing with a mastery that thrilled even while it terrified her.

He came later, after the dinner had been served and eaten, and as Elspeth was upstairs it was Colette who opened the door for him. His eyes swept over and past her with an indifference that sent the blood to her face.

'Elspeth won't be long,' she said, stepping aside for him to enter. He stood while she closed the door, his black eyes wandering round the hall. The ceiling was high and arched, the walls covered with expensive satin-effect paper. Furniture of the Georgian period was mixed with some Victorian; the carpet was Persian, the paintings by Landseer and Constable. Colette surmised that he was impressed, that he considered Elspeth to be his equal. Meriel would never have this; she declared right from the outset that he was merely playing with Elspeth, that he was not the marrying kind anyway and that if ever he did marry it would be to one of his countrywomen, a Greek who would know her woman's place as an inferior, and keep to it.

'Will you come into the sitting-room?' she invited, moving to one side of him in order to show him the unblemished part of her face. 'Mr Whitney's out, so you won't have anyone to talk to.' She was as awkward as she could be, her voice unsteady, her words scarcely making sense. 'He went out early and as Elspeth's not here, you'll have to be on your own for a few minutes.' By this time she was at the door of the sitting-room, which she opened, flicking a hand for him to enter. He was staring at her from his great height, his gaze amused, contemptuous.

'I shan't have time to die of boredom,' he said in a tone which she found most unpleasant, this in spite of the hint of an accent which she had found inordinately attractive from the first moment she had listened to his voice.

'I'll—I'll leave you th-then.' But she did not want to leave him! This was the first time she had had an opportunity to talk to him and she stood by the door, looking at him and almost willing him to speak, to take just one small degree of interest in her. 'If—er—you don't want anything?'

He frowned at her as if unable to understand what this was all about.

'What should I want?' he asked, stifling a yawn.

'Nothing,' she murmured, blushing at the snub. 'Unless you would care for a drink?' she added brightly, making one more, pitiful attempt to catch and hold his interest.

'No, thank you.' He walked to the window, turning his back on her. One hand was thrust into the pocket of his immaculate rust-brown slacks, the other reaching out to touch a Staffordshire figure of a peasant boy that stood on a pedestal by the long velvet drape.

'I'll leave you, then,' she said, forgetting that she had said this only seconds ago. 'Elspeth won't be long.'

He turned, his swarthy face a study of incomprehension.

'Is something the matter with you?' he asked with a sigh that could only mean asperity.

'The m-matter, Luke?'

He drew a deep breath.

'Is there something you want to say to me?'

She fluttered him a smile, not quite sure whether she should regard his words as encouragement or not.

'You live on an island, don't you?'

'Yes,' with a faint lift of one straight black eyebrow. 'What of it?'

She swallowed, one half of her mind wishing Elspeth would come but the other wishing she would not come for hours!

'I think living on an island must be wonderful.'

'It is, rather.'

'Much better than living here?'

'It's so different that one can't compare.' His black eyes roved, from the gleaming hair to the wide, intelligent forehead and then settled for a brief space on her eyes. She waited, watching his expression intently for the frown she knew would come when his eyes reached the unsightly blemish. He skipped over it, the frown scarcely discernible but there all the same. She tried not to colour up as he looked at the tender curves of her breasts, for a long time, she realised, wondering if he *touched* her stepsister's breasts. Meriel maintained that he touched more than that!

'He knows everything about her, you can bet your bottom dollar on that!' Meriel had said in her customary forthright way. 'She thinks she's clever, and that she's got him, but she'll learn soon enough that the Greeks never marry their "lights o' love" as they called them in the old days!'

'Is it always sunny on your island?' Colette ventured to enquire, breaking the silence.

'Not always, but most of the time. We do have seasons,' he added, his eyes still roving her slender figure.

'But it's never very cold, is it?' She stopped abruptly, swinging round as she noticed that his attention was diverted.

'Ah, Luke!' purred Elspeth, gliding into the room after standing in the doorway for a while, framed and beautiful, like a Gainsborough portrait. 'Is this child annoying you?' she added with a sudden frown. She thumbed towards the door. 'Off with you! You're in disgrace! Have you apologised to Father for your wanton behaviour?'

Colette felt a rush of blood to her face.

'I haven't—and I shan't!'

Luke gave a slight start.

'What's all this?' he wanted to know, yet appeared not to be really interested as his attention returned to the Staffordshire figure.

'She deliberately smashed part of a Derby tea-set which is of the 1815 period.'

'Not deliberately,' he corrected. 'No one would do a thing like that on purpose, my dear.'

'Tell him!' commanded Elspeth, but Colette turned and ran from the room, tears springing to her eyes. Elspeth would tell him all about it, omitting her own part in it which had started it all off in the first place. She was half way to the stairs when she halted, drawn back to the sitting-room door. It was eavesdropping, but she did not care. She had every right to know what that hateful girl was saying about her!

'She actually threw them on the floor!'

'Not only on the floor, but against the hearth. She was making sure they were well and truly broken. Dad's terribly upset; they were Mother's, you see.'

'She's jealous of your mother, is that it?'

'I've always thought so,' answered Elspeth, and Colette knew without any doubt at all that the idea had never before occurred to her, and only did so now because of what Luke had said.

'She's a peculiar girl. Has she a chip on her shoulder over that disfigurement?'

'Absolutely.' A small pause and then, with a light laugh of derision, 'She's got a crush on you, Luke. It's plain to see in her eyes every time she hears your ring at the bell, or happens to see your car turning into the drive.'

'A ... crush on me!' He laughed at that, highly amused. 'Good God! Apart from her being a green girl, there's that hideous birthmark! Does she think that I—or anyone else for that matter—would be interested in her?'

Colette turned away, her eyes filled with tears. So now she knew his opinion of her ... and it served her right, for listening.

CHAPTER TWO

MERIEL and Colette were in the canteen, chatting over their morning coffee. Colette had not by any means got over what she had heard about herself, and as she was in the habit of confiding in her friend, she had at last to tell her all that had happened after she arrived home from work yesterday afternoon. Meriel, who always seemed to be older than her years, seethed with anger and said she wished she had been there; she would have smashed all the rest of the tea-service, she said.

'And that man! Elspeth's counting her chickens, isn't she?'

'I'm not so sure, Meriel. He bought her a lovely gold bracelet last week, and she's got a lot of new clothes lately. I know she has plenty of money to spend, but I don't think she could afford those. They're all made in Paris, and I think Luke bought them for her when they were in London recently.'

'It's no proof that he's intending to marry her. They all buy their tarts clothes and jewellery. It doesn't mean a thing. I'll bet you anything you like that he's buying some other girl clothes and jewellery at the same time. He was away a fortnight ago, remember, for four days. Did he tell Elspeth where he was?'

'I don't know; she never tells me anything. In fact, we hardly ever speak these days. Oh, Meriel, I do wish I could take Mother away from that house!'

'So do I! Mum was furious when I told her that the money for your other little house was gone. She didn't believe that it had been lost in a bad speculation, but she did believe that Lewis had stolen it from her.'

'I believe it too.'

'We're having a party on the twenty-ninth of this month, Colette,' said Meriel, changing the subject. 'It's for Jane's twenty-first—oh, it's not to be anything big, of course, because we can't afford it. But Jane wants you to come.... Is something wrong?' She was sitting at a low table, her coffee in front of her, with Colette opposite. She had noticed the sudden shadowing of her friend's eyes and frowningly asked the question.

'I wouldn't leave Mother, although I'd love to come to the party.' There was a wistful note to her voice which impelled her friend to say,

'Would your mother come as well? I know my mum'd love to have her, if only to provide some help with the goodies,' added Meriel with a wry grin. 'Ask her, Colette, and let me know tomorrow.'

As Meriel had said, the party was not a big affair, but the guests were, to Colette's mind, the sort who gave pleasure, the real down-to-earth people, so vastly different from her stepfather and Elspeth, and from the people whom Elspeth frequently brought to the house. At her party a few months ago there seemed to be as big a congregation of snobs as could be found anywhere in the county. Elspeth collected them, Meriel had once said disparagingly.

'And that Greek she's crazy over is the greatest snob of them all!'

'I think you know Davy Maddox, Colette.' Meriel brought him over the moment he arrived and, recalling how he had once flattered her, Colette found herself colouring a little, at which he smiled at her in the most understanding way, holding her hand longer than was necessary and asking if he could 'book' her for supper.

'Mrs Vincent says we're having a buffet, which will be part in the dining-room and part in the hall, and she's done it like this so that there'll be room for a few small tables. I'd like to book both you and a table——' He turned to Meriel, laughing, his grey eyes open and honest, his voice gently persuasive. 'Can you fix it, love?'

'But of course,' serenely from Meriel. 'A table for two—in a cosy corner!'

Davy insisted on having the first dance with Colette, after he had helped in the rolling back of the carpet in the living-room. Jane was dancing with her fiancé, a glowing expression on her face. Colette had not had as much to do with her as she had with Meriel, there being four years' difference in their ages. But she had always liked her friend's pretty, dark-haired sister. She was not at all like Elspeth, with her supercilious ways and condescending manner of speech. Although older and far more worldly than Colette, she never once treated her with anything but the most charming cordiality, and her fiancé was the same, talking to Colette whenever he happened to meet her in town or on the rare occasion when she had been visiting her friend. Mrs Vincent would have had her often, would have been delighted to have her for tea every Sunday, but Colette wouldn't leave her mother to get the dinner by herself, and then clear away and do the washing-up.

'Enjoying it?' Davy asked half-way through the evening.

'It's super!' Colette's eyes were glowing, her face happy for the first time in weeks. 'Mother's enjoying it, too, and that's more important——' she stopped, unwilling to tell Davy anything about the life which she and her mother led up at the big house in Fairley. But it so happened that he had been asking about her and had collected quite a bit of information from Meriel.

'Your mother doesn't get out much?' he said, guarded yet with every intention of drawing Colette out.

'No, she doesn't.'

'Why?' He was holding Colette's hand, as they had just come off the dance floor. The tape recorder was starting another dance, but he led Colette away, to find Meriel and discover which table she had reserved for them.

'Well ... there's so much to do,' answered Colette as they went along.

'It seems to be a huge house—judging from the outside, and your mother hasn't any help. It's scandalous!'

Colette stopped and stared up at him, into a face that was now grave, into eyes that seemed to have a frown within their depths.

'How do you know?' she asked.

'Meriel told me——— Ah, here she is! Meriel, my love, lead us to that secluded table. We want to talk secrets!' He was in a joking mood all at once and Meriel laughed.

'It's right in the corner of the dining-room, behind those potted plants of Mum's. They looked as if they were giving up the ghost a few days ago, but Mum's done something to revive them so they make a super screen! Take some supper with you or else the best'll be gone! Try those ham and mushroom savouries; they're good—bound to be,' she laughed. 'I made them!'

'I've just seen them,' he returned. 'They certainly look good!'

He filled a plate for himself and one for Colette. There was far too much for her, but she accepted it without demur, for she was basking in his keen interest, wondering if he liked her in *that* particular way. The next moment she was hearing Luke's amused, contemptuous words and cringing within herself at the memory of her humiliation. No, Davy was just being kind; he was like that, she knew. A *nice* boy, in the opinion of most people ... not like Luke Marlis. And yet it was on Luke Marlis that Colette's thoughts were fixed for the next few minutes.

Just when she came to admit that what she felt for him was love Colette did not know, and it was only very recently that she *had* admitted it. It was something which had happened against her inclination, simply because she knew he was not a nice person, being arrogant, aware of his own attractions, of the fact that women were fascinated by his looks, his physique and his wealth. Yes, he had everything except an attractive nature, and even with Elspeth he could be caustic, treating her as if he were a king and she his humble subject. Elspeth bore it all, appearing not to be in any way put out. She was bent on marrying a millionaire, and Luke Marlis happened to be in the right category.

'It would never be a love match,' Meriel had once stated emphatically. 'He couldn't love any woman, and as for her—— Well, she's as hard as that concrete wall over there, so whoever's crazy enough to marry her'll get more than he bargains for!'

'Penny, Colette.' Davy's soft and gentle voice brought a smile to her lips.

'I was thinking about Luke and Elspeth,' she admitted. 'I wonder if they'll marry.'

He shook his head.

'From what I've heard he isn't the marrying sort. Yet most Greek men marry some time, if only to get themselves an heir. Luke Marlis is as rich as a nabob, so perhaps he will marry eventually. But it won't be to Elspeth, you can be sure of that.'

Colette said nothing. She could never have Luke herself, but if Elspeth didn't have him either she would feel far less unhappy. It was a dog-in-the-manger attitude, she freely admitted, but she could not bear to think of Elspeth marrying the man whom *she* loved.

It was well after midnight when Colette and her mother arrived home from the party and to their surprise Lewis was waiting for them, having come in twenty minutes earlier. He demanded to know where they had been, his cold eyes taking in the velvet evening dress Colette was wearing. It was a sort of Edwardian style and she had bought it in a sale. Damaged at the hem, it had been so cheap that she could not resist it even though, at the time, she had no idea when she would be able to wear it. Her mother looked pretty, too, Colette having washed and set her hair and persuaded her to put on a little make-up, and to wear a long skirt, relic of the old days when she and Colette's father used to go along to the local hop now and then.

'We've been to Jane's party,' Colette said when her mother did not speak. 'Jane is Meriel's sister.'

'You know what time it is, I suppose?'

Colette's eyes sparkled, but the retort that leapt to her lips was stilled by the imploring glance she received from her mother. She had caused enough trouble the other week, that glance said, so please don't cause any more tonight.

'We stayed to help with the clearing up,' explained Mrs Whitney, all her verve crushed beneath the hard and arrogant stare of her irate husband. 'I'm sorry it's so late.'

'But it didn't inconvenience you in any way,' Colette could not help commenting. 'You were out, Lewis, so obviously there was nothing Mother could be doing for you.'

He glared at her, his mouth tight. She looked at him and hated him—his thin cruel lips, his eyes that were—to her—like a tiger's, dangerously threatening. She hated his tallness even while admiring that of Luke, despised him for his pinchfist ways, and always she wondered what her mother had seen in him.

And yet ... what did she, Colette, see in the formidable Luke Marlis, a dark-skinned Greek with black eyes that looked right through you with indifference, a mouth that was distinctly sensuous, a jaw that spelled mastery—and God help anyone who happened to forget it! She could imagine his attitude towards those in his employ; she often fell to wondering if he had relatives—she knew he had no parents, for she had heard Elspeth telling her father so.

'This won't happen again,' her stepfather was saying in a rasping voice that grated on her nerves. 'Renie, you'll ask my permission before going out with Colette, gadding about like a young teenager. You disgrace me!'

'I'm sorry,' muttered his wife. 'I never thought to tell you I was going out.'

'To *ask* me!' he thundered. 'Ask, do you hear?'

'Yes,' replied Mrs Whitney meekly. 'I'll remember next time.'

'There won't be a next time! As for you——' he turned on his stepdaughter, eyes smouldering, 'you're too young to be out till this time of the night! In future, you'll be in the house by ten o'clock, no later!'

'I shall not!'

'Colette, dearest——'

'I can't keep silent all the time, Mother! He might control your life, but he's not controlling mine! I shall go out and come in just whenever I like!' She did not mean it, of course—or if she did it was not of any importance, since she seldom went out without her mother, and would not dream of doing so, not regularly, that was.

'You'll do as I say—or get out!' And with that Lewis turned to the door. But once there he turned again, saying to his unhappy wife, 'Come to bed at once!' And that was so significant that both Mrs Whitney and her daughter found themselves blushing.

'Don't go to him, Mother! Sleep in my room. We'll lock the door and——'

'It wouldn't do, darling,' broke in her mother bleakly. 'I suppose release will come one day——' She stopped on hearing the front door being opened with a key. 'Elspeth,' she said unnecessarily.

'At this time? Nothing's said about her late hours and she keeps them every single night!'

It was only three weeks later when Colette heard that Luke was leaving England, and she waited, scarcely able to eat or sleep, for an engagement to be announced. Luke had given Elspeth a beautiful emerald and sapphire bracelet after they had spent a week-end in Paris, and a pair of diamond earrings after they had been to London for a week. He had been there on business, and Colette ventured to ask her stepsister what his business was.

'He's in all sorts of things. He grows and exports olives and fruit; he's also in the wine business.' Elspeth as usual allowed her eyes to settle on the birthmark, but Colette was by now immune to her contemptuous stares. 'I hear you've got yourself a young man?' she added with a hint of humour. 'I can't imagine what he must be like, but there's no accounting for taste. Do I know him?'

'I don't think so.' Colette had paled, with temper more than anything else. 'In any case, you wouldn't be interested.'

'You're dead right there,' Elspeth laughed, then looked at her pityingly. 'What does he do for a living? I expect he's a labourer of some kind?'

Colette subjected her to a contemptuous glance and turned away, to help her mother in the kitchen. She was washing a huge pile of underwear and blouses which Elspeth had brought back with her from her week in London. Colette stood looking at them and could have taken them up and thrown them at her stepsister. She was becoming more and more frustrated, desperate to take her mother away from all this and yet not seeing how it could possibly be done.

That evening Elspeth seemed slightly depressed, and the reason was soon plain: Luke was not coming to take her out.

'Are you staying in?' she just had to ask when Elspeth made no move to go and change. Usually she spent at least an hour in her room, getting herself ready—'all glamoured up', as Meriel once said when she happened to be at the house when this was going on.

'Mind your own business!' was the answer Elspeth gave, and then she added, noticing Colette's clothes, 'Obviously you're going out. What's this fellow's name?'

'Mind your own business,' returned Colette, feeling rather satisfied at being given an opportunity to retaliate.

She had been keeping company with Davy since the night of the party, but they went out only twice a week. The rest of the time they spent at home, with Colette's mother, and at first she feared he would become fed up with this arrangement, but to her surprise he did not

mind in the least, accepting with sympathy and understanding Colette's reluctance to leave her mother on
her own. As both Elspeth and her father were always
out Davy did not meet either of them, nor did he want
to, he declared emphatically.

'Meriel's told me enough to turn me off,' he added. 'I
don't know how you manage to stick it.'

Colette met him that evening and they went to a
small restaurant where they had a meal. He was not
well off, working as he did as assistant in a large
departmental store in a town twelve miles away. He
lived in a bachelor flat close to his work, and he did
manage to run a small car.

'I'm comfortable,' he told her, smiling across the
table. 'I don't suppose I'll ever have much, but contentment's more important than wealth, isn't it, Colette?' She could not possibly miss the significance of
his question and suddenly all was bleak. She thought of
Luke ... oh, all the time she thought of Luke, the man
who invariably treated her with disdain, always noticing the blemish, always speaking coldly—if he spoke to
her at all, which was very seldom. Davy never seemed
to notice the disfigurement; his eyes had never once —
to Colette's knowledge—actually settled on it.

He was awaiting an answer and she managed a thin
smile as she said,

'Yes, Davy, I do agree that contentment's more important than wealth.'

'I've managed to save,' he told her, his young face
eager, his eyes clear and frank. 'It's difficult, but I made
a resolution a few years ago never to live up to my in-
come, and so, no matter what expenses come along, I
put some money away in the bank every month.'

'I wish I could,' she sighed, for the moment oblivious
of this further hint he was giving her. 'I told you about

Mother selling our house when she got married. Did I tell you that Lewis took the money and we can't get it back?'

'Yes, dear,' he returned gently, 'you did.'

'Isn't it possible to make him give it up?' Her big eyes pleaded for help. He knew how desperate she was to get her mother away from that prison she was in.

'I don't think so, Colette. You did tell me that he said the deal had gone wrong——'

'He was supposed to invest the money, not to speculate with it.'

'No, well ... he'd say it was the same thing. From what Meriel's told me about him, and from what you and your mother have let drop, I feel sure he has all the aces up his sleeve.'

'My father worked like a slave to pay off the mortgage of that house,' she said fiercely. 'Where is the justice?'

'Don't fret, darling. We shall have it sorted out in a little while.'

Darling.... She would have been blind indeed if she had not realised how this affair was going. Davy was serious, and she had already tried to visualise how she would react to an offer of marriage.

It would mean escape.... And that was as far as her mind took her before the image of a tall dark Greek intruded, blotting out all else.

Davy was helping her to vegetables from the dish which the waitress had just brought to the table. She looked at him, into a clear-skinned, honest face, into those frank grey eyes, and he smiled at her, tenderly. She swallowed. If only she could love him! If she had never met Luke Marlis. Elspeth was to blame for that— Elspeth and her father were to blame for everything!

'Enough, dear?' Davy was holding the dish, waiting for her answer. She nodded and said yes, he had given her more than enough. She watched him serve himself, thinking of the way he was with her mother—bringing her a box of chocolates now and then, or a small posy of flowers. He seemed to treat her as a mother, slipping an arm around her, and even, lately, giving her a light kiss when he said goodnight. He had lost both his parents, his father having died just a year after his mother, so he had been on his own for ten years, ever since he was sixteen.

The meal over, he took her to the car and after seeing her seated, bent and kissed her forehead before closing the door. She was lucky, she realised, having a charming young man like Davy interested in her, for she had never expected to attract the attention of any man, badly disfigured as she was.

'How about a little run out to the lake?' he suggested, but added immediately, 'Just for a short while, dear. I know you don't want your mother to be on her own too long.'

'Lewis ordered me to be in every night by ten o'clock,' she mentioned as the thought came to her.

'He ... *what?*' It was the first time Colette had heard even a trace of anger in his voice, but there was certainly anger in it now. 'He ordered? By heaven, Colette, I've a good mind to tackle him myself! Who is he to give you orders?'

'He reminded me it was his house, and told me to obey him or get out. Well, he knows I can't get out. However, as he won't be in himself until after midnight we can go to the lake. But we'll not stay many minutes.'

'He told you to get out....' Davy was at the wheel, staring at the yellow ribbon of a road bright from the glare of his headlamps. 'Get out, eh?'

They were parked in a layby at the lakeside when he said, turning impulsively to her,

'Colette, you know how I feel about you, don't you?

But you, dear—do you care at all?' His voice was strained with anxiety as he added, 'I want you to care, darling. I know you like me, but it's love I want.'

She let him take her hand, her heart heavy but yet there was a ray of light somewhere in this situation. Escape.... Both for her mother and herself.

'It's not a month yet,' she began, when he interrupted her.

'We met before the night of Jane's party, if you remember?'

She smiled and said,

'Yes, I remember, Davy, because it was the first time that a man had ever flattered me.'

'I'm glad I was the first, dear.'

She gave a sigh.

'Davy ... this birthmark——'

'Is something that worries you unnecessarily. It's not the surface that matters, Colette dear, but what's underneath. I love you and always will, and if you won't marry me I shall still be your friend, for ever. There'll never be anyone else, that I swear to you.' His voice was low and grave, and the anxiety was there, too. She wanted more than anything to say the words he longed to hear, but Luke Marlis's face was before her, arrogant, sardonically amused, challenging.

It was almost as if he were actually saying,

'You'd be a hypocrite if you said you loved him, because you love me—and you always will. I've captured you, body and soul, and you will never be free again as long as you live.'

'Davy,' Colette murmured at last, 'give me a little time, please. I suppose the——' She stopped and began again. 'I never expected any man to want me, Davy, and I'm naturally flattered. But I haven't thought deeply——'

'Don't be humble, Colette,' he broke in gently.
'You're a wonderful person in my eyes and I don't want
you to adopt an attitude of humility. If you marry me,
dear, it will be I who am honoured.'

She turned to look at him, her eyes misted over because of the deep emotion within her, and yet because
of the bleakness too, the terrible void, the hopelessness,
the drag at her heart.

'You're so marvellous,' she told him sincerely. 'I've
never met anyone as nice as you, Davy.'

'Nice....' He smiled and added, 'Only nice, Colette?'

'I did say you're marvellous,' she reminded him, and
they both laughed, easing the moment. He squeezed
her hand, then released it. He switched on the ignition,
his eyes on the lake, shining in the moonlight. Beyond
it rose the hills, with twinkling lights dotted about in
one small cluster, denoting the tiny village of Norford
nestling above the lake.

'You asked for time,' he was saying as they drove
along the road a few minutes later. 'Well, as a matter of
fact, we would have to wait a short while, because I
haven't enough money to do what's necessary. I want a
small house for us—the three of us. And there isn't only
the deposit to think of but the furniture we shall need.
However, I might be able to get a loan....' His voice
trailed away on what sounded a rueful note which impelled Colette to say,

'A loan, Davy? From whom?'

'My great-uncle.'

'Oh ... you never mentioned him. I thought you had
no relatives at all.'

'He's the only one, and not even a blood relation.
He's an old miser, living in a great mansion lying in the
midst of a huge farm. He's a gentleman farmer, in other
words, a man who seems never to mix. Mind you,' he

added with a grin, 'I can't really say anything about
him at all. All I know is that I've a great-uncle living
in Devon and he and I send Christmas cards to one
another. Nothing else! Not even a note enclosed with
the card!'

She frowned.

'Then you couldn't possibly ask him for a loan,
Davy.'

'Why? There isn't a thing to stop me.'

'He won't take any notice.'

'Ah, that's another thing altogether——' He paused
to take a dangerous bend with extra care. 'He might be
in a generous mood—who knows?'

Colette had to laugh, and she noticed how swiftly he
turned. She so seldom laughed, and so he was pleasantly
surprised, she thought.

'You're being very optimistic, Davy,' she said, specu-
lating on the possibility of his being successful. And she
had to add, a trifle apologetically, 'I haven't made up
my mind yet—you know that.'

'I understand,' he returned gently. 'I shall ask for the
loan, but even if by some miracle I get it I shan't want
you to feel obliged to say you'll marry me.'

'Thank you,' she said gratefully.

He came into the kitchen for a few minutes after
bringing her home and the three of them chatted,
Colette thinking how very pleasant it was, having someone like Davy. His presence made all the difference to
them; they seemed to forget their dejection, their
misery at the hopelessness of their situation.

But it was not hopeless any more. Colette lay in bed
that night, unable to sleep; for the future did at last
hold something—a ray of light had appeared in the
grim and empty darkness which shrouded their lives at
present. She had not told her mother of the conversa-

tion she had had with Davy, and she had asked him not
to mention his hopes to her mother.

'Not yet, Davy,' she had begged. 'Not until I'm
absolutely sure of my feelings.'

That she could never love him lay heavily upon her
and it was no use trying to tell herself that it would
not be very wrong to marry him, feeling as she did
about another man. However, nothing in her mind was
clear at present, and she only hoped that, with a little
time in which to dwell upon his offer, and to attempt to
see the future, she would be able to make a decision one
way or the other.

Neither Colette nor Meriel had expected to receive an
invitation to the wedding of their boss's daughter. In
fact, they were literally dumbfounded when, going to
their desks one morning, they found the gilt-edged
cards lying there.

'I never knew Sir Harold was even aware of our existence!' exclaimed Meriel. 'I've always believed that to
those above we were mere cogs in a great wheel!'

'I can't understand it, either.' Colette was wondering whether she could accept the invitation. For one
thing, she would feel strange among so many dis-
tinguished guests, and for another, she had nothing
remotely suitable to wear.

The explanation of the invitations came later in the
day—at lunch time in fact, when most of the staff were
gathered together in the canteen. The manager appeared and gave a short speech, explaining that both
Dorothy and her father—Sir Harold Hormbrey—had
wanted the staff to be represented at the wedding.

'The *lower* members of staff,' he went on to add. 'It
seemed all wrong that managers and other executives
should be invited, while you, who work equally hard,

and are equally important to the running of a firm like ours, should not be represented. So we devised a method of choosing which would be fair to everyone. We put all your names in a box and Dorothy drew out ten of them.'

'And to think,' said Meriel excitedly, 'that both your name and mine were drawn out!'

'I've nothing to wear, Meriel.'

'You ...? I've something, surely. We're the same size —or nearly. If you want to come home with me this afternoon we'll go through my meagre wardrobe and see what we can find. It won't be anything expensive,' she added apologetically, 'but it'll be pretty.'

'I'm sure it will,' agreed Colette, her spirits lifting at the promise, 'because you have such excellent taste, Meriel.'

'Will you tell Elspeth? Won't she be jealous!'

'I shan't say anything. They'd do something to stop me from going. The dancing's going to end very late, isn't it? I think I'll have to leave early, just to save any trouble.' Colette went on to tell Meriel of her step-father's order that she be in by ten o'clock and, like Davy, Meriel was furious.

Nevertheless, Colette resolved to be home by at least eleven, just in case Lewis should take it into his head to come home earlier than usual.

CHAPTER THREE

COLETTE did not see Luke until the guests were all in the great banqueting hall of Candover Park, the stately home of Sir Harold and his family. The wedding had gone off without a hitch, and Colette, who knew Dorothy and had even spoken to her several times when she came into the office, had gasped at the sheer beauty and elegance of the dress. Dorothy herself looked radiant, as every bride should look, thought Colette, inevitably thinking of Davy's offer and deciding that if she accepted it she would not be having a white wedding, because that would run away with money that could be used far more wisely—on the home, for instance.

She supposed that Luke Marlis must have been in the church somewhere, but as once she sat down she was too shy to turn her head, Colette had no idea that he would be at the wedding. And the reason for his being invited came as a shock to her; she supposed he and Sir Harold had done some kind of business together.

Having spotted him, Colette gave a start and Meriel, close by, wanted to know what was wrong.

'You've gone quite pale,' she added, anxiously staring into her face.

'It's ... Luke,' Colette breathed, awed by the sheer magnificence of him as he stood there, casually leaning on the long, gleaming bar that had been erected along the whole of one end of the room. He held a glass in one hand, while the other was thrust carelessly into his pocket. His interest was being held by what his companion was saying and Colette was able to stare to her heart's content, stare as she had never been able to do before.

His attire was faultless, the white shirt accentuating the teak-brownness of his skin. His black hair shone, brushed back from a forehead that was lined and dark; his height seemed to dominate the area around which he stood; certainly he towered above all the other men who were close. She noticed the arrogant set of his shoulders, the narrow hips, the leanness of his frame as a whole. The black eyes were fixed upon the man talking to him, unwavering eyes, piercing and cold as steel.

'Imagine him being here!' gasped Meriel. 'Is Elspeth here as well, do you think?'

'I haven't seen her——' Colette shook her head. 'No, she isn't, because she went out at nine this morning and didn't come back to change. I was home by lunch time, as you were, of course, but she wasn't there.'

'Well, that's something to be thankful for! It would have spoilt my day if that bitch had been one of the guests.'

Colette was still staring at Luke when another of Meriel's friends from work came up and asked her to go and look at something in the gardens. With a smiling word of excuse Meriel went off, leaving Colette standing there, quite unable to take her eyes off Luke. So it was inevitable that he should eventually become conscious of being stared at, and he turned his head, meeting Colette's eyes, his own opening wide in surprise.

He came over to her, much to her consternation, because although the outfit lent her by Meriel was charming, it was rather large, and it was also longer than Colette usually wore her clothes. She felt unutterably drab, ugly too, because of the scar. She blushed as he approached, wishing the floor would open up and she could disappear from his arrogant gaze.

'Colette! I never expected to see you here.' His eyes settled on the disfigurement and she went redder than ever. She must look awful, she thought, almost a freak with that birthmark on one side of her face, vivid purple, dark and sharply defined, and with the other cheek crimson, revealing her embarrassment at finding herself face to face with such a magnificent specimen of manhood as this handsome Greek.

'I'm surprised as well,' she faltered. 'I—never th-thought you'd—you'd——' she broke off, swallowing convulsively. '—be one of the guests.'

'I've known Sir Harold for several years.'

'Oh ... have you?'

She saw the corners of his mouth twitch, and squirmed at the idea of his finding something to amuse him about her. However, his voice was expressionless when he spoke, although that accent which to Colette's ears was so very attractive came plainly through.

'How do you come to be here, Colette?'

'I work at Hormbreys,' she answered.

'You do?' with a lift of one eyebrow. 'Elspeth never mentioned it.'

'I expect she didn't think it worth mentioning.'

'The fact that you work for the firm doesn't explain how you come to be one of the guests,' he commented, eyeing her curiously.

She told him about the putting of names into a box, adding that she was exceptionally lucky, especially as there would be over three hundred names in the box.

'It was a lovely wedding, wasn't it?' she said, overwhelmed by the interest he was showing in her. 'Didn't Dorothy look beautiful?'

'All brides look beautiful,' he returned sardonically. 'It's surprising just what you females can do to yourselves when the occasion demands it.' His eyes slid to the scar; he was thinking that in her case there was absolutely nothing she could do which would effect the least improvement.

'A girl like Dorothy doesn't need to do anything to herself,' she asserted. 'She was always pretty, judging by her photographs.'

'You've seen photographs of her?' he asked in surprise.

'When she was twenty-one—six months ago—she sent an album round for us all to see. She's like that, no edge on her. But you must have noticed?'

He smiled faintly, quaffing the rest of his drink and twirling the glass by the stem. She noticed his hands ... slender and lean.... The sort of hands that could thrill when they caressed.... She turned her profile to him, hiding the scar momentarily. She was warm inside, warm with the thoughts that would not be thrust away. She *wanted* to feel those hands on her—on her face and her throat, her breasts ... and lower. A quivering sensation affected her whole body; she had discovered a new feeling, an awareness which both thrilled and frightened her. Her thoughts switched and it was Davy's hands that caressed—— She shivered and a terrible bleakness swept over her. What was there in life for her? Oh, God, why had Elspeth ever brought this man to the house!

'Can I get you a drink?' Luke enquired, obviously becoming aware that she was without a glass. 'What will you have?'

She smiled involuntarily, every nerve affected by him, and the attention he was giving her. She savoured the moment, fully expecting him to leave her in a short

while—after he had fetched her the drink, in fact. She
said she would have a glass of lemonade, whereupon he
laughed softly and said he would bring her something
stronger. What it was she never knew; it went to her
head almost immediately and, noticing the glass begin
to shake in her hand, he took her to a sofa and sat her
down.

'I'm sorry,' she mumbled. 'I haven't had this particular drink before.'

'You haven't tasted intoxicants of any kind,' he said
in some amusement. 'In any case, you drank it far too
quickly.'

'I'm thirsty, you see.'

'Vodka isn't for quenching thirst.'

'Vodka!' She stared into the glass with a frowning
expression. 'I *thought* it tasted horrid. Meriel's had
vodka and said it was terrible.'

'I find it tasteless. However, you'd better have your
lemonade.'

She watched him walk away, arrogance and confidence in every lazy stride he took. What was it about
him that attracted her—attracted like a moth to a flame?
He was not a *nice* person; this she had said several
times before. He was too haughty, too self-assured, with
hard, noble features that might have been etched in
stone, like the faces of Greek gods carved by sculptors
of pagan Greece centuries ago. His superiority was so
marked as to be intimidating; certainly it produced in
Colette an outsize inferiority complex.

She envied her stepsister, who seemed for the most
part to hold her own with him, and not only that, but
she had the power to soften him, for Colette had seen
him actually tender with her, had noticed a smile that
was neither cynical nor sardonic, an expression that was
meant to thrill in a sort of gentle, masterly way. Al-

though Colette was ignorant when it came to love-making, she knew for sure that Luke Marlis was an expert at the art. He had not gained his reputation for nothing. He was a rake, a philanderer even here, in a country where he was a foreigner ... so what was he like in Greece where—according to Meriel, who seemed to have read extensively about that country—the men were reputed to be the most amorous in the entire world. But Colette had always held that with a man like Luke, there would come a time when he fell in love—his last love must surely appear one day—and he would then settle down to a quiet, normal existence where his wife and family were the most important people in his life.

He came back carrying the lemonade and a drink for himself, and to her astonishment he sat down beside her, asking if she felt better. Perhaps, she mused, he had felt responsible for her, having brought her a drink that almost made her tipsy.

'Yes, thank you; I feel all right now.'

'You'll have to watch the champagne,' he warned with a flash of humour which erased every hard and arrogant line from his face. 'Perhaps I must watch you myself, seeing that there isn't anyone else to do so.'

So he did feel responsible for her! He looked upon her as a child, then, she supposed with a sigh. How old was he? She surmised he was around twenty-seven or eight, but he sometimes looked older—mostly when he was appearing cold and unapproachable, with that lean jaw taut and those sensuous lips compressed. She had seen him like that once or twice when Lewis had said something which had apparently annoyed him. She had always felt that he disliked Lewis, a circumstance which afforded her a certain measure of satisfaction.

'Shall I be forced to drink the champagne?' she asked when she had tasted her lemonade.

'Of course; everyone will be expected to toast the happy pair.'

Her eyes flew to his.

'You sound cynical,' she said, amazed that she was gaining confidence sufficiently not to stammer her words.

'About marriage?' His brows lifted a fraction. 'A female's one burning ambition, and a male's downfall.'

'Oh, but   ' She frowned at his profile as he turned to acknowledge an acquaintance. 'Elspeth,' she quivered, desperate to know how he felt about her. 'She's been going out with you for some time, and——'

'Not for some time,' he corrected suavely. 'For a few months, that's all.' He sounded indifferent, she thought, and wondered how Elspeth would feel if she could hear him at this moment.

'You've bought her some lovely jewellery,' she said, not meaning to mention anything like that but it just slipped out.

'Of course,' he drawled. 'One usually does.' He was casual, glancing around, and she had a strong suspicion that he hardly knew what he was saying.

One usually does.... No mystery about words like those. Even Colette, with her scant knowledge of the ways of rakes and womanisers, had no difficulty in catching on to his meaning. She felt elated, glad that he had no intention of marrying her stepsister. He had merely used her, had fun, and when he went away it would be alone, not with a bride....

To her delight Colette found herself sitting next to Luke when, after the drinks and various savoury snacks, they were conducted into the massive dining-room where the long table was set with gleaming silver and

crystal glass, beautifully engraved by hand, with silver
candelabra and snow-white serviettes, starched and
folded like boats.

'Isn't it wonderful!' Colette could not suppress her
appreciation even though she knew the man by her
side would consider her gauche and inexperienced.
Well, she *was* inexperienced, never having had an opportunity of sitting at a table like this before. Her eye
caught his as she turned and to her surprise the contempt she expected to see was absent.

'It certainly is wonderful,' he agreed, taking the
serviette which she dared not touch and carelessly
shaking it out before flicking it across her knee.

'You, though, Luke—you're used to all this.'

'I suppose I am.'

'We—Mother and I—lived in a very tiny house before Mother's marriage.' She was talking for talking's
sake, desperate to hold his interest. This was her finest
hour! She had him all to herself for a little while. Her
whole world was rosy ... and suddenly she knew that
pretence was her aim. She would pretend that he was
her young man—no, her lover, and her friend.

'So Elspeth told me. Are you happier now than you
were then?'

The question, coming unexpectedly, brought her
head round swiftly.

'Why do you ask, Luke?'

He was silent a moment and then,

'Your stepfather's a hard man.'

'Is it so obvious?'

'Very obvious,' he answered.

But Luke could be a hard man, too, decided Colette,
though she felt that he would only be hard to those
people who deserved the treatment, whereas Lewis was
inherently hard—no, cruel was a better description.

The first course was brought—shrimps Mariette; this was followed by potage St Germain, and then fish. It was all very leisurely, with wines to wash down the seven delicious courses. Colette, watched carefully by her companion, touched very little of the wine. He did not want to carry her home, Luke told her laughingly ... but she could think of nothing she would like better than to be carried in his strong arms!

The dancing began soon after the meal was finished, but by now it was already getting late and Colette felt she ought to be leaving in a little while. But she was having a thoroughly wonderful time, with Luke dancing with her in spite of the fact that she protested at first, stating firmly that she could not do the steps. He insisted, and with surprising patience took her round the floor. She then danced with one or two other young men, but later found herself once again in Luke Marlis's arms.

'It's hot in here,' he said, flicking a finger across his brow. 'Let's go outside for a few minutes.'

She stared up into his handsome face, scarcely able to believe her ears. Was he really inviting her out into the garden? With racing pulse she allowed him to conduct her to a door and from there to a room with a balcony. From the balcony they descended a flight of marble steps to find themselves in a secluded part of the gardens. She said nothing when he began to walk to the dark places, but to her disappointment he did not stop at all. It was merely a breath of fresh air he wanted ... not a kiss or embrace. ...

Back in the garden proper she could smell roses; the air was heady with the perfume and she stopped by a border, to touch the velvet petals of a blood-red bloom.

'Roses don't often have scents these days,' she said, 'but some of these have. Can you smell them, Luke?'

'Yes, very nice.' Absently he reached out and snapped a stem, then stood twirling the rose between his fingers. Colette stood beside him, watching his profile, which was taut now, hard and forbidding. Within her, feathery ripples were affecting her nerves, creating a desire that in turn affected her senses. The setting was romantic, the stars like diamonds glittering from a bed of deep purple velvet and the moon like a hammock in their midst. She touched his arm, then ventured to touch his hand. He turned, and she sensed that he was frowning, and suddenly she was conscious of the scar, of her own inferiority, and she withdrew her hand as if she had touched something hot. Luke tossed the rose away and said abruptly,

'Come along! It's getting late. I'll see you home——' He paused a moment. 'Or have they transport laid on for you?' he asked.

'No—er——' If only she could have lied! He would have taken her home in his big car. But she could not lie and she added that there was transport laid on by the firm.

He was walking away, ahead of her; she turned back, looking for the rose and, spotting it lying there on the grass, she stooped and picked it up.

'You dropped your rose,' she said a trifle breathlessly as she came up to him again. 'It's a shame to let it die.'

He glanced down at it in some surprise.

'Keep it,' he said carelessly. He seemed to consider her to be slightly mad for bringing it to him. 'What on earth would I want with it?'

Keep it. . . .

She was still pretending. He had given her a rose . . . and roses were for love. . . .

It was after twelve when they were leaving the reception, and Colette, for whom the time had sped on golden wings, went white when she saw the clock.

'Lewis will—will....' She tailed off, terror on her face.

'What in heaven's name is wrong?' Luke asked impatiently. He appeared to have had enough, seemed so bored that all he wanted was to get away from her as quickly as he could.

'He told—ordered me to be—be in for ten o'clock,' she faltered. They were in the hall and all around them guests were chatting in groups prior to departing. The bride and groom had left over three hours ago, for the airport where they were to board an aeroplane for Paris.

'He *ordered* you——' Luke was obviously sceptical about this. 'Why would he want you in at ten?'

'He says I'm too young to be out after that.'

'At seventeen? In my country, yes, most certainly you'd not be allowed out, not by yourself at all, in fact —but here——' He shrugged and said that her stepfather's attitude was ridiculous.

'He takes it out on my mother.' Tears started to Colette's eyes and with a little childish gesture she fetched a hand across them, preventing the tears from falling. 'Will—will you please come with me, Luke?' she implored. 'He won't be able to—to say anything if —if you explain.'

Luke frowned and shook his head.

'If he knew you were coming here then he must know you'll be late home.'

'He doesn't know I was coming here.'

'You didn't tell him?' he said, staring in surprise.

'No—you see, he wouldn't have let me come—— At least I felt he'd do something to prevent it.'

Luke turned at that moment as someone he knew stopped to bid him goodnight, and as the two chatted for a space another precious few minutes went by.

'You'll be all right in the works car,' he said when eventually he turned to her again. 'I don't feel like driving very far tonight.' He was indifferent, and slightly annoyed at her timidity. He would have no patience with cowardice, she thought, wishing she could make him understand that it was not cowardice but the desire to avoid dissension, and to make things less troublesome for her mother at the same time.

'I would be very grateful if you'd come with me.' She was holding the rose and he glanced down at it, a sigh escaping him when presently he agreed to take her home.

But if he had believed her to be putting on an act he was to discover his mistake. Both Lewis and his daughter were up and waiting when Colette rang the bell. And almost before the door opened Lewis was demanding to know what she meant by staying out till this time.

'You've been with some man,' he snarled, 'and up to no good! Well, miss, I warned you—and now you can pack your bags and get out—this very night!'

'Lewis,' cried her mother, 'you can't turn her out at one o'clock in the morning. . . .' Her voice trailed as she caught sight of Luke. He had come up in the darkness, a few paces behind Colette, his original intention being to leave her once he saw the door open. But he had overheard her stepfather and now he was on the top step, unceremoniously brushing him aside as he walked into the hall.

'Colette *has* been with a man,' he said icily, 'you are right. She's been with me——'

'With you!' from Elspeth incredulously. 'I don't believe it!'

'Colette was invited to a wedding,' explained Mrs

Whitney. 'I've been trying to tell you, Lewis, but you wouldn't let me speak. She——'

'Mrs Whitney,' interrupted Luke with quiet authority, 'I shall do the explaining.' And he proceeded to do so, aware of the glinting expression in Lewis's eyes, and the hostile and vicious one in the eyes of his daughter.

'You've been with one another all afternoon and—and night?' Elspeth's voice was unsteady. 'But you said, Luke, that you had some business to attend to, and that was why you couldn't take me out——' She broke off, gritting her teeth at the idea of Colette's hearing her speak like this. 'You,' she snarled, pointing a finger at her, 'you deceitful wretch! You never even mentioned any invitation to a wedding—and you must have had it some time——' Again she stopped, a look of bewilderment on her face. 'How do *you* come to be invited to the same wedding as Luke?' No one answered her and she stormed on, driven by fury and jealousy into repeating herself, unable to control her vicious tongue even though she must have known she was damaging herself in Luke's eyes.

He was regarding her with the utmost contempt, but he said nothing to her, addressing himself to Lewis, telling him firmly that Colette was not to blame for anything.

'I kept her,' he lied finally. 'She wanted to come home hours ago, but there was dancing and I made her stay.'

'You ... made her ... stay?' from Elspeth slowly, her mouth twisted to an ugly curve. 'You wanted to dance with *her*! Why, you've never had any time for her! You've remarked over and over again about that scar——'

'That's enough!' he broke in roughly. 'I wanted to

dance with her because there was no one else there whom I knew——'

'You could have taken my daughter,' interposed Lewis softly. 'You must have been able to get her an invitation to this wedding.'

Luke seemed likely to explode.

'For God's sake, let the matter drop! Colette is not to blame! Have you got that?'

'Very well.'

Everyone looked at Lewis as he said this. Colette knew without any doubt at all that he was merely putting Luke off, that, realising he was lowering his dignity, and that Elspeth was lowering hers, he wanted only to have Luke off the premises.

'You're not going to punish her in any way?'

'No, Luke, not now that you've explained.' Still quiet ... insidiously so! Colette and her mother exchanged glances and both knew that of all the quarrels they had had with Lewis and his daughter, there had never been one as serious as this.

'I'll go, then.' Luke turned to Elspeth and said casually, 'This will have to be our goodbye, I'm afraid. I leave England in five days' time. And as I've a great deal to do between now and then, I shan't have any time to spare. Goodbye, Elspeth.'

She stood rooted to the spot, her face purple with fury, unable to believe what she had heard. Colette thought of what Meriel had said—that Greek men never marry their mistresses, and she wondered how Elspeth had not known this. Perhaps she had, but was hoping that she would be different from the rest of Luke's lady friends. Perhaps she had cherished the idea that she would be his last love ... the one whom he would marry.

No sooner had the front door closed upon him than

both Lewis and Elspeth turned on Colette and her mother. Abuse and recriminations flowed from their wrathful tongues, and the end of it was that Colette was told to leave first thing the following morning.

'You're responsible for breaking up Elspeth's romance,' Lewis said, 'and we don't want you here any longer.'

'I shall go with her!' cried Mrs Whitney, even while knowing full well that it was impossible.

'I don't think you will,' returned her husband confidently. 'Colette doesn't earn enough for one, let alone two.'

He still was unaware of the rise. But even with that Colette knew she would have difficulty in maintaining herself, chiefly because of the price of flats. True, she could go to Meriel's house. Her mother would welcome her, but Colette was not leaving her mother here alone —not after a scene like this.

And so her thoughts turned to Davy, and now her mind was straight. She knew what she must do, knew that there was nothing else for her but marriage to a man she did not love.

CHAPTER FOUR

THE sun was rising over the hills, painting the landscape with saffron and gold and delicate shades of peach. Colette stood by the window for a few moments before turning to smile at her husband.

'Many happy returns,' he said. 'Have a wonderful year, my darling.'

She went to him and, sitting on the edge of the bed, caressed his forehead, and drew her fingers through his thick fair hair.

'I'm bound to have a happy year, aren't I—having you?'

He closed his eyes, then opened them again.

'Dearest Colette, why should I be so lucky? Tell me that.'

She laughed and got up; the long leisure-gown fell in drapes about her slender body and she heard Davy catch his breath.

'We've been married for over three whole years,' she remarked, looking down at him and liking the way his hair was ruffled.

'Well, that's a fine piece of eloquence, my love. I would like to know how we could have been married for three years that *weren't* whole!'

Again she laughed and said teasingly,

'I stressed the *whole* just to make sure it registered that it's a long time.'

'You mean: it seems longer than that? My girl, if you're trying to tell me you haven't been happy all that time I shan't believe you.'

Her eyes were still staring into his. She said softly,

'I have been happy, Davy—thank you, darling, for everything.'

'No, dearest, it's I who must thank you. You've made my life a heaven on earth.' He got up and kissed her tenderly. 'There's only one thing that didn't come out right, isn't there?'

She smiled gently and lifted her lips to his again.

'It's in the hands of the gods,' she said. 'If we're to have children then they'll arrive—some time.'

'There's nothing wrong with either of us.' He gave a small sigh, but the next instant he had shaken off his dejection. Davy was always like that, Colette thought. So calm about everything, so resigned to whatever fate meted out for him. She had made him happy, supremely so, and he would never ever know that she did not love him. She had lied from the first, but had no regrets or sense of guilt either. She was as happy as she expected to be, and her mother was happy too, loved as much by her doting son-in-law as by her daughter.

'We're a happy family,' she murmured, speaking her thoughts aloud. 'We're fortunate, Davy.'

'Indeed yes, and in more ways than one.' He moved away, towards the door leading to the bathroom, but on reaching it he turned. 'Who'd have thought that old Uncle Patrick would turn up trumps the way he did?'

'He did so much more than you asked.'

'I asked for a loan, that was all. You could have knocked me down with a feather when he offered me the management of his estate and a lovely house to go with the job!' He went into the bathroom and she listened for him running the water.

She turned, her pensive gaze on the antique dressing-table that had been in the house when they took it over. It looked quite ordinary—beautifully carved, with four drawers along the front. But one day when she was polishing it Colette had discovered one of those little secret drawers which were often put into a piece of furniture of this kind. She glanced at the closed door of the bathroom, listened again and then, reassured by the rush of water going into the bath, she went to the dressing-table and, pressing a button inside one of the other drawers, pulled at what appeared to be a small panel—one among several identical panels—and opened the drawer. From it she took a tiny book of poems, which she opened to reveal a rose, its petals dull brown and thin, like paper. She recalled with poignant intensity the day she had pressed it. It was the day she had told Davy she would marry him, the day after the wedding.

A rose which she had pretended had been given her by the man she loved. A rose from Lucifer....

Reverently she put it to her lips. Would the day ever dawn when she would throw it away? she wondered. It was silly and sentimental to keep it, and to bring it out like this once or twice a year. She was twenty-one today, old enough to have more sense, old enough to admit the folly of wasting her love on a man who, by now, would have forgotten she ever existed.

'Darling....' She turned guiltily on hearing Davy's voice from the bathroom.

'Yes?'

'There isn't a bath-towel in here.'

'There is, in the cabinet. I put it there to warm for you.'

'Bless you!'

At breakfast both her husband and her mother gave her presents, a lovely gold locket from her mother and a pearl necklace from Davy.

'They say pearls for tears,' said Davy as he fastened the necklace for her, 'but that's rubbish. These are for smiles, my love ... smiles for the rest of your life.'

'They're beautiful! Oh, Davy, thank you so very much!' And then she turned to her mother, thanking her a second time for her present, and finally declaring herself to be the luckiest girl in Devon.

'Are you going over to see Uncle?' her husband was asking later, when the daily woman had arrived and was seeing to the carpets. For some reason she could never explain, Colette had always disliked the sound of a vacuum cleaner. Davy grinned and thumbed as he added, 'It'll get you away from that.'

Patrick Blane's home was one of the most beautiful in the county. It was faded and carried an air of general neglect, as was to be expected when its owner had never been married, and had lived there for over forty years, ever since he inherited it from his father. He had a housekeeper, Maisie, a hefty Scottish woman who would never tell her age. Davy teased her, saying she was almost as old as her employer, and all she would answer to this was that she was as old as her tongue and a bit older than her teeth.

'You're a lot older than your teeth,' he would declare, but that did not help him to discover her age.

She opened the front door to Colette, then told her to go into the drawing-room, as Mr Patrick was expecting her.

'Ah, there you are!' he greeted her, smiling and indicating a chair close to where he sat, by the large french window. 'So you're twenty-one today. A wonderful age, Colette—and you're a wonderful girl.'

She smiled and the colour fused her face, Uncle Patrick, like Davy, never seemed to notice the blemish, and gradually she was beginning to admit that, to those who really mattered, it seemed to be nothing.

'How are you this morning?' she asked, a trifle anxiously because of late she had noticed a change in him, very slight, and neither her mother nor Davy had noticed—or if they had, they'd made no mention of it to her. But she had noticed a bluish tinge around his mouth, a tiredness in his eyes, which at the best of times were watery and half-closed.

'I feel all right, my dear, but it can't be denied that I'm getting old, and none of us can live for ever.'

'Don't,' she admonished, pained. 'If you feel off colour let me get the doctor.'

'I don't feel off colour. Haven't I just said that I'm all right?'

She smiled and changed the subject.

'Davy and I were saying this morning how lucky we are to have the house, and for Davy to have such a good job. You know, Uncle, when I agreed to marry Davy I expected us to be poor all our lives, and instead we're rich.'

'Not as rich as you will be one day. No, you're merely comfortable at present.' He paused, as if having a little difficulty with his breathing. 'When Davy wrote asking for that loan I thought at first I'd write and tell him to go to the devil, but then I thought to myself, it was silly not to give him something now, seeing that I'd recently made him my heir.'

'He didn't know that at the time.'

'Of course he didn't. I'd never had much to do with him and I'd left it all to charity. But then when he asked for the loan, saying he wanted to get married, something of a benevolent nature got into me——' He broke off, laughing ruefully. 'I said to myself I'd better take a look at this young fellow I'd made my heir, and so I sent for him. He brought you as well——

Now, my memory's going a bit, and I can't remember if
you'd lost your father or something—— No, it was your
stepfather—he'd thrown you out. Well, his loss was my
gain. I loved you, Colette, on sight, and that was why
I never hesitated to do all that for Davy.

'And now,' he added, rising from his chair and reaching for the walking stick that was leaning against it,
'I've something for you, something which I've been
keeping for your twenty-first birthday. They came with
the house and farm, when I inherited them, but these
jewels have been in the bank for many years. I had
them brought to me and now they're to be yours.' He
was walking towards a large painting as he spoke and
Colette watched, fascinated, as he swung it aside to
reveal a safe. Two or three minutes later she was staring down at several velvet-lined jewel cases, her eyes
boggling at the incredible beauty of a necklace of
diamonds and sapphires with a bracelet and earrings to
match, an emerald bracelet, a pair of diamond drops
with matching star for her hair, and the last case contained three rings—a diamond solitaire, a ruby surrounded by tiny pearls and an eternity ring.

'They—they can't be—be for me!' she gasped. 'Uncle
Patrick, I'd be scared to wear them!'

'Nonsense, child. They're well insured. Such things
as these are for showing off, not putting into the bank
or a safe.' He took up the necklace. 'Here, put it on——'
He stopped, noticing her fingering the pearls Davy had
bought her. 'That's new, isn't it?'

She nodded, amazed that he should know the necklace was new. But right from the first he had been surprising her one way or another. Davy declared that it
was knowing her that had made him human.

'Davy bought them for me. Aren't they lovely?'

'Very pretty, and they suit you—but I never did care

for pearls,' he added frowningly. 'Small seed pearls are all right, but——'

'And Mother bought me this locket,' she said hurriedly, wanting to change the subject because she herself had never really cared for pearls, mainly, she knew, because of that stupid saying, 'pearls for tears', which her husband had mentioned when he gave them to her. She withdrew the locket from inside her blouse and showed it to him. 'I wanted to wear both presents,' she admitted a little deprecatingly, 'and so I have to have Mother's inside my blouse because it would look too much if I wore the locket as well as the pearls.'

He gave a small sigh, looking at the jewellery and lapsing into a thoughtful silence.

'I oughtn't to give you these just yet,' he mused. 'But I'd certainly like to.'

Colette said nothing. The jewellery was lovely, but she could never see herself wearing any of it. For one thing, there would rarely be an occasion for which it would be suitable, not as far as she could see.

'Take it,' decided Uncle Patrick at last. 'I'm sure neither Davy nor your mother will mind.' He looked at her and smiled affectionately. 'They know you well enough to be sure you'll love their presents just as much as mine—more, probably,' he added with a rueful glance. 'You have all your values right, my dear.'

She averted her head, embarrassed as always by his flattery. She had brought joy into his life, he had often told her; Davy did not know how lucky he was.

'Do—do you want me to take them now, Uncle?' She could have left them here, but she felt he would be hurt if she suggested it. Where would she put them for safety? The secret drawer? She shook her head automatically. There was one treasure there, and although she knew it was silly and futilely sentimental, she could never bring herself to put anything else with the rose.

It was less than a week later when Maisie, distressed but practical, phoned through to say that the old man had died during the night.

'He expected it,' she went on to tell Davy. 'And I don't think he minded, because he's been saying lately that he's very tired.'

'He went peacefully,' Davy told his weeping wife. 'Don't pine, darling, for according to Maisie, it does seem to be what he wanted.'

She nodded, believing this to be true, but she knew Uncle Patrick's death would leave a terrible void in her life. He had been such a dear friend, the man to whom she took all the minor worries and problems which unaccountably came to her now and then. And one day he had said, his eyes alert, perceptive as they looked into hers,

'You have a secret, my child . . . a deep, deep secret, in your heart. Do you want to tell me about it?'

She had not denied she had a secret, because one never lied to a man like Uncle Patrick, but she had said apologetically,

'I can't tell you about it, Uncle—not you, or anyone.'

'It makes you sad at times.' A statement which again she did not contradict.

He was gentler than ever with her after that. He had her come to him every afternoon for an hour so, and would repeatedly apologise for not having them all to live in the big house, but said that he was an old man set in his ways and much as he had come to love them all he jibbed at having the smooth pattern of his life upset. With Davy he was like a father—or perhaps grandfather was a better description of the way he treated him, with more indulgence than a father would. With Colette's mother he was kindness itself, having been told by Davy of the terrible life she had led with her second husband and his daughter. Uncle Patrick wanted to know about these two, and Colette had, over the three and a half years she had known him, told him just about everything. He asked if she had ever seen them since, but she said no, nor did she ever want to again. She thought of the lovely house that went with her husband's job and often wondered what Elspeth would think, could she see it.

But the 'big house' was fit for royalty, or so Colette thought. She loved the high ceilings with their delicate plasterwork, the beautiful French furniture in some of the rooms, the fine old clocks and china cabinets, the exquisite marquetry, the glistening chandeliers, and above all she loved the gardens with their statuary and miniature lakes, their flower-borders and sweeping lawns. It was all rather neglected even now, for Davy was always busy looking after the farm and had little time to spare for what the old man considered to be less important things.

'When all this belongs to you and Davy,' Uncle Patrick would say, 'you'll have it looking spruce again.'

They moved in two months after he died, letting their own house to Philip Grady and his wife Susan, both of whom worked on the farm, Philip as a most efficient and conscientious cow-hand, and his wife in the huge hothouse in which was grown many out-of-season luxuries, and especially flowers, which both Susan and Colette loved to cut.

Uncle Patrick had left the estate to Davy, but with substantial legacies to Colette and her mother.

'If Lewis could see us now he'd gnash his teeth in fury,' Mrs Whitney said as she stood in the centre of her lovely bedroom, watching her daughter fix the drapes to her satisfaction. 'I never thought that you and I would live like this.'

Colette smiled as she turned.

'Nor did I, Mother.'

'It was a lucky day for us both when you married Davy, wasn't it?'

Colette nodded, her eyes far away.

'Yes, Mother,' she agreed quietly, 'it was.'

She looked at her, marvelling as always at the difference both in her appearance and her mentality since, on the engagement of her daughter, she had left her husband for ever. She was young again, and happy. She would never know the cost to Colette, or suspect that tears were occasionally shed for what might have been, had she, Colette, been beautiful like her stepsister, and had Luke fallen in love with her. The dreams—impossible dreams—came unbidden, and Colette would allow herself to be carried away by them, living for a few blissful moments with the man she loved, feeling those strong arms about her—as she had when on that unforgettable night he had danced with her—feeling his body close to hers. And in her dreams she would go further, because dreams were part of her precious secret and she could put them away, along with the rose, and no one would know they even existed. She never felt guilty about her dreams; she had been a good wife to Davy, who had never for one moment suspected that she did not love him. He was the luckiest and the happiest man in the world, he often told his wife, which made her content, and grateful for the ability to hide from him that which would have shattered his happiness for ever.

Uncle Patrick's car was a very early Buick which had, since the arrival of Davy on the scene, been kept in immaculate condition. He had been allowed to drive it, but only when they took the old man out, for he seemed to have an affection for it out of all proportion. He treasured it, and Colette would often tease him when, of an afternoon, she would see him by the open garage doors, standing there staring at it fixedly.

'How's your baby today, Uncle Patrick?' she would say, laughing.

'Envious brat!'

'Can I drive it? Davy's teaching me.'

'No, you can't. I don't mind Davy; but no woman touches that car.'

'It was thick with dust when we first came!'

'I admit it. That fellow who did the lawns reckoned he'd keep it clean, but he soon got fed up.'

Colette had smiled. Much as she loved him she was under no illusions regarding his generosity—or rather, lack of it. He would never employ two people where one might do, and so many things had become neglected, including the vintage car. Davy had been shocked, and the moment he had time to spare he got down to polishing it. And his reward had been those rare occasions when his uncle would ask to be taken to town, perhaps to the bank, or he might even ask to be taken for a run, just for the sake of riding in it. But during the last year of his life he had lost interest, and although Davy would have liked to use the car he did not even go as far as to ask permission.

However, it had been left to him, so now he was the proud owner.

'It's not for using all the time,' he told his wife. 'We've got the other car for everyday use; this one's for special occasions. If I can find the time—one day—I shall take part in a rally.'

Meanwhile, he took them out in it occasionally, and

one lovely afternoon in June, when the countryside was bright with colour, Mrs Whitney suggested a run.

'I know you're busy, dear,' she said to Davy, 'but to take an hour off won't do you any harm—in fact, it'll do you the world of good.'

He agreed, and got the car out.

'I feel like the Queen in this car,' enthused Mrs Whitney. 'These old ones have something the modern ones will never have.'

It happened instantaneously; the impact was never even felt. All Colette knew was that one moment the road was a smooth white ribbon bordered by trees, and the next it was blacked out because consciousness had left her.

She came to in a hospital theatre, bewilderedly aware of clinical smells and white walls, of ghostly figures flitting about, silently, as if death were close before them. She heard whispers, and then the subdued tinkle of metal against metal. Blackness again, then light. It all seemed to happen in seconds when in reality the operation—which was to be the first of many—had taken all of three hours.

It was over a week later that she was told the truth. Before this they had merely said that her husband and mother were dangerously ill. She herself was too ill to feel anything but a vague disquiet about their conditions. And then it was decided that she was able to stand the shock. She could only stare, even then, at the white-clad figure who in gentle accents had told her that both her husband and her mother were dead, that they had been killed instantly when the Buick hit a lorry out of control, which emerged from a blind turning.

'Both....' she murmured frozenly at last. 'My—my

husband—and—and my mother?' She shook her head
against the pillow and experienced an unfamiliar stiff-
ness. Her head and face were heavily bandaged; she was
told of the two operations she had had, one on her head
and one on her face.

Two days later her thoughts were clearing sufficiently
for her to absorb the real impact of what had happened,
to dwell on the tragedy, to realise that she was now
totally alone in the world.

'Why wasn't I taken as well?' She spoke to the doctor
when he came round to see her, in the small private
ward where they had put her after the operations, the
second of which took place within hours of the first.
She had been at death's door, she learned afterwards;
they had had little hope of success with the operation
on her head.

'You've been a very lucky young lady,' she was told
much later, when the bandages were off her head.

Lucky. . . . She still wondered why she had not been
killed as well, for there was nothing to live for now.
The surgeon, Mr Cummings, told her with infinite
understanding that she would not always feel like this.
She was young and she'd get over it eventually.

'And the birthmark you had will be gone,' he added,
but at that time Colette cared little about whether it
would be gone or not.

Maisie came to see her regularly, and so did some of
the workers on the farm. Philip had taken over the
management and none of the others appeared to have
shown any resentment.

'It was the obvious thing to do,' he told her. 'Your
interests must be taken care of, Mrs Maddox.'

Her interests? It had not registered at that time that
she was now a wealthy young woman, possessor of a
large estate and prosperous home farm. It was only as
the weeks passed that it began to take root in her mind,

and she would turn frozenly into the pillow, wishing she could exchange it for the lives of those who were lost.

Davy, so gentle, with never a wrong word for anyone; her mother, who had suffered under the harsh domination of her husband.... Both dead, taken long before their time.

'I don't want to live,' she told Mr Cummings again, after another operation where skin-grafting had taken place on her face. 'What is there for me now?' Her eyes implored and, frowning, he looked away. She was asking for a drug ... to put her to sleep.

'You're depressed, and it's only natural,' he said, but added once again that she would not always feel like this.

'Time is the infallible healer,' he assured her, and although at the time she had scarcely listened, so lacking in interest was she, it was later borne in on her that the surgeon with his wide experience had known much better than she.

It was over eight months later that the last of the cosmetic surgery took place; the transformation had been gradual, with a ghastly scar at first where part of her face had been damaged, but a miracle had been performed and she knew that her stepfather and Elspeth would not recognise her now.

'We had to give you a new nose, I'm afraid,' said Mr Cummings with a smile. 'I hope you'll come to like it.'

She could not make out what had been done. All she knew was that the face that looked back at her from the mirror was beautiful, but the knowledge gave her scant satisfaction. If only Davy could have seen her, and her mother who had always grieved over the disfigurement.

Her thoughts rarely went to Luke these days; they

were too occupied by the tragedy. But time passed and she found herself becoming interested in the estate, helped enormously by the faithful Philip and Susan, and in the house by Maisie and the two daily women whom Colette had employed immediately she and Davy and her mother had moved in. It had been so hard for Maisie, who could not possibly cope. Now, the whole house shone; silver and brass got cleaned, antiques polished, and the dust removed from rooms that had been closed up for years.

All this helped in the healing process, but even after three years Colette was still listless at times, and eventually Maisie suggested she take a holiday abroad.

'Go somewhere exotic,' she recommended. 'The West Indies or the Far East. What about Bali? I've read about it and it must be beautiful. A man was talking about it on the radio last week and I thought of you. He declared it to be the most idyllic spot in the whole world.'

'I wouldn't care to go alone, Maisie.'

'These days people think nothing of it. Think about it, anyway, and if you do decide we'll get Philip to contact the travel agent for you.'

Much to her own surprise the idea took hold, with the result that Colette eventually found herself actually favouring it.

'I think I shall take your advice, Maisie,' she decided, hoping she was not acting impulsively. 'I'll go off somewhere—but where, that's the problem. I know I should hate being in an hotel all on my own. I *have* thought of a cruise, and perhaps a short stay somewhere afterwards.'

'A cruise would be the very thing! You're sure to have plenty of company on a big ship. As for staying. . . . Well, you'd be in an hotel, which you've said you wouldn't like.'

'Not for a long stay—no, I wouldn't like it then. But for a short stay——' She stopped, unable to understand why, after her initial reluctance to go away, she now wanted to go away for a long time, to get right away from this huge house and the responsibility of running it. It had occurred to her to sell it, but always there was the conviction that neither Davy nor Uncle Patrick would have liked to think of strangers coming into possession. Another deterrent was that Colette did have company here, and plenty to occupy her mind, which she would not have in a smaller place which had no farm attached. Yet she did want to get away, and she did also want to be free to stay away for as long as she liked. 'I'll take a cruise initially,' she told Maisie, 'but after that I shall travel a bit—— It's all very vague,' she added, 'but the thing is that I don't want you or any of the others worrying if I'm out of touch for a while.'

Maisie frowned and shook her head.

'I can't say I like that idea,' she protested. 'How shall we know what you're doing or where you are if you don't keep in touch?'

'I shall be all right. I'll send you cards.'

'It sounds funny to me, Colette.'

'I expect it does,' agreed Colette with a wry expression. 'I'm awfully vague about it all. I'd like to go away and forget this place for a while, that's all.'

'Well, it's your own decision,' said Maisie resignedly. 'It's not for me or anyone else to tell you what to do.'

The ship docked at Barbados for eleven hours. Colette, looking exceedingly bronzed and healthy, went ashore with a young couple she had become friendly with on the day the ship left Southampton six days previously, and they hired a taxi which took them on a tour of the island before returning them to the ship in time for dinner. The ship docked at other islands in the Caribbean, then docked finally at Port Everglades from where those who wanted could fly back to Southampton, while others had the option of staying for a week at a luxury hotel on Miami Beach. Colette had booked the latter when she booked the cruise, but before the week was up she had booked another cruise which was to take her, finally, to Genoa. From there she travelled to Venice, sending postcards now and then to Maisie and to one or two of the other employees on the estate. She found she was enjoying cruising and seeing something of the world. It was all new and although she naturally felt lonely on occasions she did have company for most of the time. She stayed only two days in Venice, being lucky enough to get on a ship cruising the Mediterranean. It called at several Greek islands, and it was only to be expected that she would consult the large map provided and look for the island of Attikon.

The ship went close.... It actually docked at the island of Skiathos, she was told by the Purser, who handed her a brochure so that she could look for herself.

Skiathos was not very far at all from Attikon, but the ship was not scheduled to stop at the smaller island. She wondered if Luke was still living there, and if so, was he in residence or was he away on one of his business trips? It was almost eight years since she had last seen him, she reflected, surmising that, in his mid-thirties now, he would look different, older and more mature. He was probably married with children—— She cut her thoughts abruptly, and angrily, resolved never to let his image trouble her again. It was ridiculous! At almost twenty-five she ought to have more sense!

When the ship's fire siren was heard most of the passengers thought at first that it was a rehearsal.

'But it hasn't been announced,' said the young woman who had tacked herself on to Colette and seemed determined never to let her out of her sight. 'It's usually in the news sheet we get put under our cabin door every morning.'

'It's a real fire!' someone shouted, but at that moment the Captain's voice was heard, calm and quiet, informing the passengers that a small fire had broken out in the engine-room. It was nothing to worry about, but of course everyone must collect their lifejackets and make their way to the particular station that had already been allotted to them. There was a general rush for the stairways, and a small amount of panic from the very young and the very old. The young woman who had attached herself to Colette bemoaned the fact that they were at different stations and said that as the fire was being effectively dealt with—if the Captain's word was to be taken—then they should keep together until it was seen whether or not they were ordered to take to the lifeboats. But Colette shook her head, pointing out that in an emergency like this the advice given them at the fire drill must be followed, for otherwise all order would collapse.

She went swiftly to her cabin to collect her lifejacket, but to her horror she encountered smoke the moment she emerged. Was the situation more serious than the Captain would have them believe? It struck her that he would never reveal to the passengers that it was a dangerous situation simply because such information could cause wholesale panic. What must she do? Her heart was racing as she stepped back into her cabin, the smoke already having got into her throat. Trembling from head to foot, and with her lifejacket in her hand, she went through the door once again, realising that to stay in her cabin was to cut off all escape should the corridor become blocked. The idea of running through the smoke occurred to her, and she was about to do so when to her dismay she saw the flick of a flame through it. The other way! She ran even while aware that there was no exit that way; she was merely running from the smoke and flames towards a dead-end!

'Oh, God help me!' She was terrified, trapped! She recalled reading about a ship that caught fire and because the precautions had not been adhered to the passengers were unable to get to the boats.

She stopped and looked back, deciding there was nothing for it but to take a chance and race through the smoke and what little flame she could see. It might be coming from one of the doors along the corridor, in which case all might be clear once she had got herself past it. The decision made, she acted on it instantly and to her relief she was correct in her guess that the smoke and flames were issuing from one of the doors. But the next moment she was facing a wall of flames, with no possibility of getting through it. She could hear screams and shouting, officers giving orders, the clanking of metal ... and the crackling of burning wood. She turned again, instinctively putting distance between her and the oncoming conflagration. The heat was terrible; she ran into her cabin, suffocated by smoke and by the excruciating pain in her chest, result of running but of fear as well. The window! Her eyes dilated as she looked at it. Her cabin was in fact one of the most expensive staterooms on the ship, and although she had only a porthole in the bathroom there was a proper window in the bedroom. How to break it! She hammered on it and by some miracle a member of the crew happened to glance towards it. Within seconds he had seized an iron bar and she stood back as he smashed the window, fumbling with her lifejacket as she watched him. She was through just as the flames lit up the open doorway of her cabin ... through but still trapped. The crew member who had smashed the window for her was nowhere in sight and she thought, in the panic now assailing her, that he must have jumped overboard. All around were flames and smoke; before her was the sea, with lifeboats everywhere, and some people swimming about, people who had obviously jumped overboard. She heard a shout from somewhere.

'Jump, you fool! Jump before it's too late!'

She stood, every nerve rioting, her legs so weak that she doubted if she would have the strength to jump overboard. There seemed to be small boats of all shapes and sizes coming out from a dark and nebulous shape in the sea ... an island! Yes, because she saw light twinkling from what must be a steep hillside.

'Jump!' The voice was harsh with urgency. She still had no idea where it came from, but as the heat began to scorch her back she fixed her lifejacket and jumped, bracing herself for the shock of impact with the water. She felt it drag her down, but the next moment she was floating, held by the lifejacket she had almost forgotten to put on properly. Within minutes she felt strong hands supporting her and realised that someone was swimming close to her. A voice encouraging her, telling her she was quite safe. Another voice from a boat....

She was hauled on board, holding on to consciousness only by the greatest effort, for her head was spinning and it would have been so much easier to have let herself drift into oblivion.

'Easy now,' said the first voice. 'You've nothing more to worry about. Just relax.'

She turned to look at the man who had saved her ...

turned to see, by the light of the boat's lantern, the face of the man whose voice she had already recognised.

Luke Marlis....

She tried to utter his name but failed. Her throat felt as if someone had callously pushed a rasp into it, and her tongue was swollen. She was aware of the burning pain in her back, of the fact that all around her there was chaos, that Luke Marlis had dived overboard again, and another man was urging her to sit down. She obeyed, hearing herself say,

'Whose boat is this?'

'It belongs to my cousin—Luke. He saved you—well, he brought you out of the water. I don't expect you would have drowned, not with your lifejacket on and all those people and boats around. How do you feel? Pretty shot at, I reckon.'

'Yes——' She eased her back away from the support of the bench she was on. The man saw her flinch and asked if she had been injured.

'My back—it's nothing, really, but it was so hot.'

'You must have been pretty close to the fire?'

'I w-was....' To her dismay she started to cry. Reaction, she excused herself, brushing away the tears as she saw her rescuer holding someone else aloft for his cousin to haul aboard. It was an aged lady she had spoken to once or twice. She was scarcely able to breathe, but seemed incredibly calm once she was on the boat and seated by Colette.

Another passenger was eventually brought aboard and by that time there was no one else in the water.

'Let's go,' from Luke in a brisk businesslike tone. 'The sooner we get these people into dry clothes the better.'

CHAPTER FIVE

THE small boat seemed to pull in at a private jetty where Colette, along with the other two, was helped from it and then guided to a dark path. She was shivering, and almost in a state of collapse from shock, and when she stumbled she felt herself swept up into a pair of strong arms and carried with the utmost ease towards a wide floodlit archway which was the side entrance to a luxurious Greek villa with a shady courtyard to one side of it. She was carried through the courtyard into the villa and there received by a maid in black who was told to take her up to the 'guest suite'. She turned for an instant to glance at Luke, and to say shakily,

'Thank you—thank you very much.'

'Don't mention it,' he returned suavely. He had not recognised her, but she did not expect him to.

Her heart was racing all the time she was in the bathroom, being helped out of her wet clothes by the maid, whose name was Androula. To be in Luke's house.... How unpredictable was fate, to bring her here after all those years!

'Your back, miss—it is of the red colour.' Androula spoke English very well but with a far more pronounced accent than her employer.

'It happened before I'd managed to get my lifejacket on. It's nothing.' No, it was nothing compared what it could have been, thought Colette, shuddering at the memory of being trapped, and of resigning herself to being burned to death.

'All your clothes haf gone,' said Androula unnecessarily. 'But it is a terrible thing that happen!'

'I was very fortunate.'

'Ah, but yes! My master he go as soon as the distress
—the distress—signal——?' She looked askance at Colette, who nodded immediately. 'My master very good at
the swimming, you know. Very good—*poli kala*!'

'The other two people,' said Colette, dropping her
underwear into the bath. 'Are they here too?'

'I think somebody else take them in. Here we haf not
very much rooms—only one guest suite, you know!'
The girl, dark-skinned and smiling, shrugged her shoulders expressively. 'My master he only by himself, but
sometimes he haf friends who haf this suite.'

'I suppose everyone living on this island will be taking in people from the ship,' commented Colette, obeying the girl's gesture and standing under the shower
which Androula had brought to the correct tempera-
ture.

'I think this is so, because the hospital here on
Attikon is too small—very much too small.'

Colette faced the spray, unable to let the warm water
go on to her back. Androula had left the bathroom, but
she returned when Colette was drying herself, some
clothes over her arm.

'Mine,' she said deprecatingly. 'They too big, I think,
no?'

'I'm very grateful for them,' returned Colette, managing a smile.

'The undies—this is what I hear the Anglais say for
this article.' Androula handed over the article in question, then tights and a bra. A white blouse beautifully
embroidered came next and lastly a flowered cotton
skirt. 'You look very nice—*poli kala*!' She went to the
dressing-table and picked up a comb. 'If you like to
use? Your hair is wet, but I haf drier if you like?'

'No, thank you, Androula, I'll just give it a comb through for now.' Colette was desperate for a drink and asked for a glass. Androula said at once that her master was expecting his guest to go down for supper when she was dry and changed. 'It is very late, but he haf no dinner because of the ship, you know. He will be hafing a bath and then his supper.'

'I see....' Of course, she had expected to be seeing him, because when he had handed her over to Androula he had said,

'I'll be seeing you later. Androula will show you where to come.'

'I take you down to the dining-saloon if you are ready, miss?'

'Yes, I'm ready.' She glanced into the mirror and marvelled that she could look so well after that terrifying experience. And she looked beautiful.... Yes, even though her hair was wet and rather straggly.

Luke was in a casual outfit of light grey slacks and a short-sleeved shirt; his hair, thick and black but with a few threads of grey at the temples now, was brushed back from his lined forehead. He had changed little; there were a few lines at the corners of his eyes, but that was all. His features were the same, sharply etched and arrogant, his manner suave and yet coolly superior. But the contempt Colette had once known was not in his eyes ... nor was the indifference she had so often encountered. On the contrary, he was regarding her with exceptional interest, his black eyes appraising every feature, examining every curve, stripping her, almost. She coloured in the most attractive way and lowered her long, curling lashes so that the amber glow from the wall light above her, and to one side, made shadows that seemed to fascinate him and she could sense his desire for her to look up at him again. Instead, she broke the silence, to thank him once more and to ask about the others who had been in the boat.

'They've gone to my cousin's house,' he answered, his eyes still on her face. 'What is your name?'

She hesitated, glancing at him, and said in a husky voice,

'Jennifer.' It was Meriel's other name and as a little girl Colette had loved it, wishing she had it too, instead of just the one name, Colette.

'Jennifer?' he frowned. 'It doesn't suit you.'

She gave a slight start but managed to laugh.

'I'm sorry, but one can't help one's name, I'm afraid.'

'And your other name?'

'Maddox.'

'Jennifer Maddox.' His black eyes slid to her left hand. 'You're married?' His voice was sharp, she thought, and a frown had knit his brow.

'I'm a widow.' She was cool, serene and unemotional on the surface, but her heart was beating far too fast. This man could still affect her ... she still in love with him.

'A widow?' he echoed incredulously. 'But how old are you, for heaven's sake?'

'Twenty-four—almost twenty-five.'

'Good lord! You look about eighteen!'

She was parched and just had to ask for a glass of water.

'Have something else. Lemonade? We grow our own citrus fruits here, so you'll like it.'

'Yes—thank you.'

'Have a chair. Are you hungry?'

'Not very.'

'You've had dinner——? No, you can't have, surely?'

'The alarm went off just before we were to dine.'

'Then you must have something.' He had poured the

drink and he brought it to her, bringing a small side
table with him and placing it at her elbow. Colette
glanced round the room, remembering that he was
reported to be a millionaire twice over. Everything
spelled luxury, from the deep-pile carpet to the cut
glass chandeliers hanging from an exquisitely-painted
ceiling. No expense had been spared and yet there was
about the room an air of casual elegance that meant
comfort—a lived-in atmosphere. 'Supper will be served
in about five minutes,' he was saying. 'It's really dinner,
but my man assures me it's been spoiled by the delay
and he's doing something with it and calling it supper.'
A smile of amusement touched the fine outline of his
lips and she caught her breath. He attracted her as
much as ever. She sighed inwardly, cursing the fate that
had brought her here, to be affected by him as strongly
as before—this when she had decided never to allow his
image to trouble her again.

They went into another room for supper, a beautifully appointed dining-saloon where they were waited
on by a stocky Greek manservant called Davos, a stolid-
faced man who reminded Colette of the typical English
butler whose face would crack if he tried to smile.

'Georgios has said that the meal is spoiled, Mr
Lucius.'

'I expect it will be palatable,' returned Luke, who
had obviously instructed his servant to use English
during supper. 'Georgios knows he's a genius, and that
everything will be all right.'

Colette was seated opposite to him; she saw his eyes
upon her repeatedly, knew he was interested and
thought: he hasn't changed. He's still a rake. He wasn't
married, obviously, but she surmised he would have a
lady friend. The Greeks could not do without them,
she had heard on the ship. But of course she had heard

it before, years ago, when he was going out with Elspeth. Colette was intrigued by the fact that he had never married, though. For surely he would like to have a son, someone to inherit his great wealth?

'Tell me about the ship,' he invited when the first course was put before them. 'What happened? Do you know what caused the fire?'

Colette shook her head.

'No, none of us did. We weren't troubled at first because the Captain sounded so calm.'

'He'd be trying to avoid panic. The ship's not blazing now, by the way. They've got the fire completely under control.'

'Will the company send out another ship at once?' she asked anxiously. She wanted to get away from here, escape before Luke's magnetic personality played havoc with her feelings all over again.

'They should do, but it all depends if they have one. It's a busy time of the year.'

'But some other company——' She looked at him with sudden suspicion. 'They can't leave us all here for any length of time!'

The black eyes roved.

'Have you commitments?' he asked, a strange inflection in his voice.

'Well ... no,' she answered truthfully.

'So it won't inconvenience you if you don't get back yet awhile?'

Colette looked at him, nerves tensed. She knew what she ought to say, if she were wise. What she did say was,

'Not at all.'

He picked up his fork, drawing a breath.

'You would be more than welcome to stay here, as my guest,' he said. '*Epitrépsaté moo nà sàs proskalésso.*'

'What is that?' she asked, colouring up.

He laughed.

'You took it for a very different kind of invitation. However,' he added in some amusement, 'I merely *invited* you to be my guest.' A pause, with his fork still poised. 'Will you, Jennifer?'

'I don't even know you,' she murmured awkwardly, looking down at her plate of smoked salmon.

'That can easily be rectified.'

She frowned at him, vitally conscious of his draw for her, his fatal attraction. It was plain what he wanted from her. Nevertheless, she found herself saying,

'Why should you want me to stay here, in your house, when we're complete strangers?'

'I like you,' was his swift and bland admission. 'I want to know you better.'

'You amaze me,' she gasped. 'Do you usually want to know strange women better?'

At that a smile of amusement touched his mouth.

'Depends on whether or not they're beautiful ... and desirable. You are both.'

So this was how he made his approach. Had he adopted this same line with Elspeth? If so, then she must have known from the very first that his intentions were not serious.

'You're trying to flirt with me, Mr ...?' She glanced at him. 'Your cousin, on the boat, said your name was Luke, but he didn't mention your surname?'

'Luke will do very nicely,' he assured her with the glimmer of a smile. 'You say it most attractively.'

'Don't you think we'd better tackle this?' she suggested. 'Your servant's ready to serve the second course, unless I'm very much mistaken.'

'Davos will serve the second course when he has my orders to do so,' he returned coldly. 'My servants don't take liberties with me; they know better.'

Colette felt snubbed and glanced down, attending to her food. He was no different! All the arrogance was still there. But of course there *was* a difference: he found her attractive, was willing to have an affair with her ... for how long? It was a fascinating point, and when she had recovered her composure she heard herself say,

'You'd like me to be your guest, you said? For how long?'

She looked at him with interest, a smile hovering on her lips.

'Now that,' he returned with a speculative glance, 'is not a question I can easily answer.'

'Because you have no idea just how long it would be before you became bored with me?'

'You've obviously grasped my meaning,' he applauded. 'For a moment I'd begun to think you were innocent in the ways of men like me.'

'Rakes, you mean? Womanisers? I assure you I am, Mr—er—Luke. You bewilder me with the pace you take.'

He gave a crack of laughter.

'You're a girl after my own heart! As for the pace you mention—well, I'm direct; there's no sense in taking the devious path and wasting time in the process.'

It was Colette's turn to laugh. A rake he might be, but in this half-jocular mood he was inordinately attractive!

'You're very glib,' she accused. 'I shall turn down your kind invitation and stay at an hotel.'

The black eyes held humour.

'Do you suppose you'll find a room in our one hotel, at a time like this, when we've four or five hundred extra people on our island? We don't cater for tourists,

Jennifer, so you'd have difficulty at any time, but now....' He shrugged expressively and cut himself a piece of salmon. 'No, my child, you really have no alternative than to accept my—er—kind offer, as you call it.'

She changed the subject.

'Do you ever go away from Attikon?' she enquired, feeling specious but enjoying herself for all that.

'Often. I've business contacts all over Europe.'

'In England?'

'Of course.'

'Shall you be going soon?'

'Not for a couple of months at least. Why do you ask?'

'Just interest,' she answered casually.

'What part do you come from?'

'Devon.'

'A beautiful county.'

'You know it?' Colette put the last piece of salmon into her mouth and sat back, alert to his keen gaze, conscious of her straggly hair but at the same time conscious of her beauty.

'I've been there a few times.' He lifted a finger arrogantly to bring his servant to the table. Colette thought: this is the East, where servants and women know their places. 'Whereabouts do you live in Devon?'

'Twenty miles from Exeter.'

'Tell me about your home.' He watched Davos pick up his plate first, then ordered him to put it down again.

'You go to the lady first,' he said shortly.

'But——' Davos seemed amazed by the order. 'Very good, Mr Lucius, I take the lady's plate first.'

Luke turned his attention again to Colette.

'How long have you been a widow?' he asked.

'Over three years.'

He said after a pause,

'What happened?'

'It was a car accident.' She became guarded, dis-inclined to answer further questions, but he was in-sistent, with a faintly domineering manner which she found it difficult to ignore.

'He was killed.' A statement, before he added slowly, 'You were in the car, too?'

Should she confess who she was—telling him about the operations which had transformed her features as well as taking away the birthmark? Would he lose in-terest in her if she did tell him? Would she care if he lost interest? She had no intention of becoming his intimate girl-friend, so it did not really matter if he did lose interest. And yet ... she hated the idea of his losing it; desperately she wished to hold his interest, his admiration for her looks. She frowned inwardly, wish-ing she knew what she wanted, but her brain was a whirlpool of questions she was powerless to answer. But there did emerge this profound desire to hold his admiration for as long as she could.

A sort of panic took possession of her; she felt that if she admitted she was in the car Luke would ask more and more questions until at last he would have the whole story from her. And so she lied, saying no, she was not in the car.

'But my mother was,' she added, her lips quivering at the memory of her terrible loss. 'Both she and my hus-band died instantly.'

'And you were left all alone in the world....'

To her astonishment she saw a dramatic change come over his face, saw a softness, a compassion of which she would never have believed him capable. A strange and most pleasant sensation swept through her, a sudden

warmth that dissolved all tension, a heightened awareness of the love which had never faded through all the
years.

He was staring at her so intently that for one frightened moment she felt he had recognised something
about her, that he was trying to place her, but the impression passed as a slow smile broke the fixed reserve
of his features.

'You're too young and too beautiful to spend the
rest of your life in widow's weeds,' he declared at last.
'You must learn to live again ... and to love.'

To love? How little he knew!

'I'm not wearing widow's weeds,' she denied. 'Time is
the infallible healer, as everybody knows.'

'What made you come on this cruise?' he wanted to
know, watching Davos approach and stop uncertainly
by the table. An arrogant flick of Luke's hand and
the man moved, quickly, to serve Colette first.

'I wanted to get away,' she answered truthfully. 'My
housekeeper suggested it in the first place and the idea
took root. I went to the Caribbean first, then stayed in
Miami. After that I was in Genoa and Venice, and then
I decided to take a Mediterranean cruise.' And found
herself here, with the man whose admiration she had
never even hoped to gain. No, not in her wildest
dreams.

'You must have plenty of funds,' he commented.
'Your husband left you comfortably off, apparently?'

She nodded.

'Yes, he did. His great-uncle left him a large and
important estate. It all came to me.' She thought of her
jewellery, which she had left in the Purser's office for
safe-keeping and wondered if it was still there or if it
had been lost in the fire. It seemed unimportant; she
was alive, and that was the only important thing ...

alive and sitting here, dining with the handsome Greek who, at one time, was as unreachable to her as the stars.

Elation filled her, joyful elation born of a simple happiness. She had her values right, Uncle Patrick used to tell her, and she saw now that he had spoken the truth. She valued this interlude of friendly conversation and the candlelit dinner shared with Luke. It was something to remember in the future, when he and she were miles apart ... when she went to her secret drawer and took out the rose.... He was watching her with the most odd expression and she fluttered him a lovely smile, her beautiful eyes glowing in their dark frame of thick curling lashes.

Luke caught his breath; she heard it distinctly and then there was silence, intense, a vibrating silence which neither seemed able to break. It was the man-servant who did eventually break it by saying,

'Shall I pour some more wine, Mr Lucius?'

Impatiently he shook his head.

'I'll do it myself, Davos! That will be all. Come back when I ring and not before.'

Rising from his chair, Luke took the wine from the ice-bucket and filled Colette's glass. He was stooping over the table, close to her; the silence was again intense as he turned his head, deliberately bringing it close to hers. She sat erect, tremblingly aware of what was to come even before she felt his lips on her cheek ... the cheek that had once been so disfigured by the birthmark. Feathery ripples raced along her spine and she was caught in a web of emotion that allowed no pretence and found herself lifting her beautiful eyes to send him a look of glancing tenderness. His eyes widened, then became veiled. Replacing the bottle in the bucket, he took her face between the palms of his hands and kissed her on the lips.

She coloured delectably, her eyes shining, her whole being yearning for his embrace, for his caresses and his intimate love. Where was she heading? Was it the wine which robbed her of her senses? Or was it the magic of the setting, with flickering candles in their gleaming silver holders, and flowers tempting with their heady perfumes? She decided it was a mixture of them all ... but mostly it was the power this man had over her had always had over her even when he did not even notice her. Yes, mostly it was Luke himself, the dark formidable Greek in whose veins ran the blood of pagan ancestors, worshippers of gods like Lucifer....

'Eat your dinner, Jennifer.' His voice was low and gentle; Colette could not believe this was the cold austere man she had once known. Had he been like this with Elspeth? If so, it must have been a terrible blow when he had so casually told her that the affair was at an end.

If she had an affair with him would it end the same way—with him becoming tired of her? Colette could not imagine such an eventuality, then assured herself that her refusal to admit it stemmed merely from vanity.

'Luke,' she said timidly after attempting to eat her dinner as he'd told her to, 'I'm not hungry.'

'Then leave it, my child. Do you want to go to bed?'

She nodded, aware that a heavy weight of tiredness had descended upon her in the last few minutes.

'It's been quite a day,' she told him ruefully.

'Quite a day,' he agreed.

'I'll wait until you've finished,' she smiled. 'I haven't finished my wine yet.'

'Drink it slowly, then.'

'It's nice ... smooth....'

'Child, you're falling asleep!'

She shook herself and sat up straight.

'No such thing,' she denied.

'Twenty-five, you say.' He shook his head in slow motion, a half-smile on his lips. 'You're just a babe. I don't believe you're anywhere near twenty-five.'

She looked at him with a sort of happy tiredness and murmured,

'A woman never puts up her age, Luke. You don't know anything about them if you think for one moment that I'd say I was twenty-five if I wasn't——' She stopped and frowned at him. 'I'm twenty-four!' she corrected indignantly.

'You're tipsy,' he told her with a wry grin. 'Do you realise my child, that I shall have to carry you to bed?'

'Oh. . . . I think I would very much like that.'

'You ask for it,' he told her severely. 'Shall I seduce you?'

The wine had certainly done something to her.

'I don't believe you're a man like that, Luke,' she stated, and he burst out laughing.

'My dear Jennifer, all men are like that!'

'Jennifer?' she repeated, frowning. 'Who's she?'

He stared, the laugh dying on his lips.

'You're Jennifer. You told me that was your name.'

'Jennifer. . . .' Suddenly her head cleared. 'Do you like my name, Luke?'

His eyes had narrowed.

'Is that your name?' he wanted to know. 'I've already said it doesn't suit you.'

'I'm sorry you don't like it. What name do you like?'

'It's high time you were in bed,' he decided firmly, and got up from his chair. 'I'll take you up, and finish my supper afterwards.'

He carried her as if she were a doll; she rested her head on his shoulder, put her arm around his neck.

When he entered the bedroom he put her down on the sofa by the window.

'I'll send Androula up to you,' he promised. He looked down at her, lying against the cushions, a lovely slender girl whose face was flushed and whose eyes sparkled. 'It's a pity you drank too much wine——' He stopped, correcting himself. 'It's a pity that it went to your head, because if it hadn't——' He broke off and shrugged. 'Maybe I'm a fool,' he said, 'but my conscience forces me always to play fair in a situation like this.'

CHAPTER SIX

SHE awoke to an instant sensation of excitement and the quickening of her heartbeats. Her swift-winging thoughts took her to last night, to a romantic supper for two beneath a high ornate ceiling from where crystal chandeliers hung, unlighted but gleaming in the light from the candles beneath, on the table, where silver candlesticks were just a part of a beautiful picture of elegance and good taste. The place mats and coasters were also of silver, and the wine-cooler too, the glasses hand-engraved, the napkins beautifully embroidered. Perfumed flowers added an exotic air of romance, and from somewhere unseen there had drifted to her ears the sad, soul-stirring strains of *bouzouki* music.

Luke.... He had found her attractive! The enviable position which she had once resignedly accepted to be the right of girls like Elspeth was now hers!

It had been inevitable that, for these past three years, since the transformation brought about in her appearance by modern science, she would notice that men's stares were now admiring as they passed her in the street, whereas before, she was subjected to vacant looks, as if the men were trying to be kind and pretend they hadn't noticed the ugly blemish, or looks of pity, because here was a girl who would never get a man. She recalled Elspeth's enquiry as to what her young man was like. She had never met Davy, had never known of the marriage because, the morning after that dreadful scene, Colette had gone to Davy and, between her sobs, had poured forth all that had happened. He took her back, and with a quiet dignity told her stepfather that he was taking her away, and her mother too. Elspeth had not been there; Lewis had scarcely looked at Davy, had not asked where he was taking them, or what his intentions were. But he was furious when, as they were packing while Davy waited outside in his car, he stormed into the bedroom he shared with his wife and actually threatened her with violence. If she went she'd never get a penny from him! She'd come crawling back. There was a lot more contained in the tirade, but it fell on deaf ears. Davy was willing to take them to his little flat and to Colette and her mother at that time it was a haven protecting them from all further hurt and humiliation.

Very soon afterwards came Uncle Patrick's offer and from then on life was smooth and happy. Colette, resigned to a life without loving, accepted her lot with a sort of quiet philosophy, grateful for what fate had given her, and she vowed never to hurt Davy by letting him know, by one small act or sharp word, that she did not love him. He had asked her if she did love him, of course, and she had astounded herself by the ease with which she was able to lie.

But through the years secret tears had been wept—not often, and never lasting long—and she would go to the secret drawer and take out the rose, remembering that Luke had not picked it specifically to give to her, but she had pretended that he had. She smiled now as she recalled those moments of pretence on that evening when for the first time she had been in Luke's company, dancing with him, sitting by him at the table. Seventeen.... She had come a long way since then, had acquired a dignity all her own, was a wealthy woman ... and she was attractive to the man she loved.

Could she make him love her? To her mind there

was almost always that 'last love' of song, for it was natural for a man to settle down eventually, and to have children.

She sighed, drawing up her knees as she sat leaning against the pillows. She hugged them and rocked a little, her eyes dreamy, one half of her mind now and then straying, so that she caught glimpses of that terrible scene on the ship, and later, in the water. But the other half of her mind was on Luke, and the unmistakable interest he had shown in her.

She slipped out of bed, staring at herself in the long mirror and deciding that Androula had excellent taste in nightwear.

She went to the window and drew back the curtains. The sun was coming up, over the horizon, spreading a panoply of brilliant flame through to deepest crimson bordered by gold and amber and flaring bronze. Where was the ship? It dawned on her that she was at the wrong side of the house to see it. How had the firefighters fared? Luke had seemed to think that the ship had been saved; he also thought that everyone had escaped in the end. Colette hoped this was true, and the casualties would prove to be no more than superficial injuries, and perhaps shock.

She would know later, but for the time being she wanted to wash her hair and take a bath. Her back was still rather painful, but had not been really burned, though the dress she had been wearing was scorched.

In the bathroom she noticed with a smile that Androula had provided just about everything she could possibly need, from a bottle of shampoo to talc and body lotion and, folded neatly on a chair, her own underwear, laundered and pressed. Her shoes had been dried and were in the bedroom, she had noticed, so there would be no need for her to wear the sandals provided last night by Androula.

It was over an hour later that the Greek maid knocked on the door and entered the room carrying a tray.

'You are up!' she exclaimed. 'I think I not come yet because you be sleeping long time today after tiredness last night. But you up and dressed!'

'And I've washed my hair,' smiled Colette, eyeing the contents of the tray. She had hoped to be having breakfast with Luke.

'It is beautiful—the golden hair, I think. I haf of the black hair and it no good!'

'It's beautiful,' corrected Colette. 'You should be proud of your hair.'

Androula's face brightened, and her swift smile revealed a flash of a gold tooth.

'You like it? My friend haf hers—what you say in Anglais ...?' Androula laid down the tray on a small table by the window and turned, her brow creased as if she were in some sort of pain. 'I not know this name for making hair white—light—in the colour.'

'She had it bleached, you mean?'

'That is right! She haf it bleached and then made red!'

'Good heavens! Did it look awful?'

'She like it, and her husband like it as well. It dark red, like leaves when they sometimes die.'

'Russet, you mean.'

'Russet ... russet. . . .' Androula looked at her, a smile in her dark eyes. 'I like this name what you say. It is red?'

'Dark red, like the leaves when they die.'

'I remember this. My friend will like to say her hair is of the colour russet!' Androula began to pour some tea into a cup. 'It is only morning tea, miss,' she said. 'Mr Lucius say that if you are awake and would like to haf breakfast with him he will wait for you.'

Colette's heartbeats quickened.

'Please tell him I shall be down in five minutes.'

'I do that,' smiled Androula. 'You look beautiful, miss. My master he like beautiful girls all the time.'

Colette watched her leave then picked up the tea she had poured. My master he like beautiful girls *all the time*. He had many, then? One at once or several? Perhaps he had a girl-friend here, on the island ... or perhaps he had more than one.

She went from the bedroom and was immediately approached by Androula who took her to the breakfast-room. Luke was standing by the window, gazing out to where the white cruise ship lay anchored, looking so regal, and so safe. . . .

He turned as she entered, his black eyes roving from her face to the gentle swell of her throat, and down, to the firm contours of her breasts, where they stayed, and she coloured, feeling naked under his all-examining stare.

'Good morning,' he said. '*Kalimera!*'

'Good morning,' she returned shyly.

His fine lips curved with amusement.

'Too shy to say "good morning" in my language?'

'Is that what it means?' She advanced into the room and stood by a chair, her hand resting on the back.

'Yes, that's what it means. I never come out with anything suggestive first thing in the morning. Sit down, my child, and relax. Or have you a hangover from last night?' He was pulling out a chair for her. 'No, that was ungallant of me! You look beautiful, Jennifer. Your hair is glorious.' He flicked a hand imperiously; she obeyed the unspoken command and advanced towards the chair. As she lowered herself into it he made sure she had to come close to him. She felt his chin deliberately touch her hair, and then he had

Yours
FREE.
Love beyond Desire

A compelling love story of mystery and intrigue... conflicts and jealousies... and a forbidden love that threatens to shatter the lives of all involved with the aristocratic Lopez family.

Now...you can bring romance into your life, every month, with a subscription to **SUPERROMANCES**, the almost 400 page romantic novels. Every month, three contemporary novels of romance will be in your mailbox. Twice as thick. Twice as much love.

SUPERROMANCES...begin with your **free** *Love beyond Desire*. Then month by month, look forward to three powerful love stories that will involve you in spellbinding intrigue.

SUPERROMANCES...exciting contemporary novels, written by the top romance novelists of today. And this huge value...each novel, almost 400 pages... is yours for only $2.50 a book. Hours of entertainment for so little. Far less than a first-run movie or pay-TV. Newly published novels, with beautifully illustrated covers, filled with pages of escape into a world of romantic love...delivered right to your home.

Bring twice as much romance into your life, beginning today. And receive *Love beyond Desire*, **free.** It's yours to keep even if you don't buy any additional books. Mail the postage-paid card below.

SUPERROMANCE
1440 South Priest Drive, Tempe, AZ 85281.

← Mail this card today for your FREE book.

A compelling love story of mystery and intrigue...conflicts and jealousies...and a forbidden love that threatens to shatter the lives of all involved with the aristocratic Lopez family.

Mail this card today for your FREE book.

grasped a handful of it, tugging it gently so that her head was tilted backwards and she was looking up into eyes that were faintly mocking ... but there was triumph there too, as if he were feeling very sure of a victory in the near future.

'Do you always have breakfast so late?' she asked, breaking the spell with the prosaic enquiry.

'No, but I waited for you. What do you have? *Borò nà sàs prosféro: liga froóta?*' He stopped and laughed. 'Can I give you some fruit to start with?'

'Yes, please.' She was given grapefruit which had already been prepared. After that Luke rang a bell to bring Davos to him. Eggs and bacon were brought, and toast. Colette asked if Luke had heard anything about the disaster and he said his cousin had rung earlier to say that apart from some injuries to a number of passengers there were no serious casualties.

'The ship's in a pretty bad mess,' went on Luke, passing her the toast-rack. 'But the damage appears to be much less severe than it might have been. You'll probably be able to get your clothes, later. We'll go and see what we can do.'

'The smoke and flames appeared to be coming into my cabin when I left it,' she said. She had already told him how she managed to escape, told him last night in the course of conversation.

'Well, it isn't important. We'll soon get you fixed up with clothes.'

She lifted her chin, a gesture that caused Luke to open his eyes wide, then narrow them again.

'I don't want you to be buying me clothes. If as you say the ship isn't damaged too much then the Purser's office might have escaped. If so, I can get my money and my jewellery.'

'What do you think you can do with jewellery? Pawn

it?' He shook his head, his expression one of amusement. 'No pawnshops here, I'm afraid.'

'I can get money,' she assured him confidently.

'But not at once.' He passed her the butter, his eyes roving, appreciative. She seemed to fascinate him, she thought, her hopes soaring. Would she be his last love?

It would be a miracle, but miracles did sometimes happen. 'For the present, my dear, you will have to let me help you.'

She said nothing, feeling that she'd not gain anything by argument with a man as masterful as Luke Marlis.

'This housekeeper you mentioned,' said Luke when, the meal finished, they were sitting with their last cup of coffee. 'She'll be anxious about you?'

'I told her I'd be travelling around, so she won't really be worried. I sent her a card from Rhodes when we called there but didn't say I was on a cruise. She won't know I was on that ship—— I expect it will be in the news?' She looked at him enquiringly and he nodded his head.

'I expect it'll be in the world news, yes. Shall you send her a card from here?'

'I think so.'

'And tell her you're staying for a while?'

'I haven't made up my mind to stay for a while,' she told him.

'I invited you to stay, remember?'

She made no immediate answer and for a space the only sound to break the silence was that of the drilling of cicadas in the jacaranda trees outside the open window.

'I could stay,' she murmured at length, lifting her eyes to throw him an anxious glance. 'But I believe you haven't told me exactly what my—er—position will be?' It was with some considerable difficulty that she managed to get these words out, and even then she was painfully aware that they were not at all well chosen. The sudden twitching of his chiselled mouth only served to strengthen her conviction that she had been far from diplomatic.

'What you are really asking,' he said with some amusement, 'is whether I want you as my lover or not. The answer's simple: yes, I do.'

Colette blinked and gasped. She had learned last night that he was an outspoken man, but never had she expected him to speak quite as bluntly as this. Where was the romance she was seeking—the magic and the tenderness? This offer he was making savoured of the cold and practical, a sporting challenge to a girl who, he obviously believed, had been starved of sex for over three years and would therefore not only gladly accept his offer but would probably be grateful for it into the bargain. She wished she could be angry with him, or haughty, giving him the cold shoulder—or even, to use a phrase she abhorred, to tell him to 'get lost'!

She was unable to do any of those things, because her heart was saddened by hopelessness. What price her ambition when he was telling her, with a sort of amused yet callous indifference for her feelings, that his only interest in her was desire for her body?

Better that she leave here, before temptation in all its force should crush her ideals ... and sully her dreams.

She said with a determination that surprised her,

'I won't stay here tonight. There must be accommodation to be had somewhere on the island. I know I ought to be grateful for what you did—when I was in the sea—and in fact I am grateful, and I thank you again. I thank you also for this hospitality, but——'

'But you do not thank me for offering you more than

hospitality?' The amusement was no longer there. On the contrary he was frowning a little, and she was sure there lurked a trace of disappointment in his eyes. 'Money and jewellery usually do the trick, but unfortunately for me you appear to be wealthy in your own right.'

'That is immaterial,' she was quick to assure him. 'Even if I were a pauper I'd still have no interest in your suggestion.'

His frown deepened.

'You're on your own,' he said. 'You've no man-friend at home——'

'How do you know that?' she queried.

'Because you'd not be doing all this travelling. You were bored with your life, the routine and total lack of excitement, so you thought you'd use a little of your money to see something of the world, of life——' He looked at her straightly. 'I'm right, so don't deny any of it.'

'I wasn't intending to. You're very clever,' she added, reflecting that once—eight years ago—she could never have begun to hold her own with him as she was doing now.

'Not clever, just perceptive. You're a fool, girl! Life is for living and you're a long time dead! You're a long time old as well, so grasp your pleasure while you're young—and beautiful.'

She brought down her lashes; his gaze was far too intent for her to hold it.

'You sound as if you have lived your life to the full,' she said, picking up her cup and regarding the pattern of gold and green on the side of it.

'I have my moments,' he returned casually. 'A lovely woman has always been a challenge to me.'

Faintly she smiled.

'You obviously consider me beautiful——'

'I've never met a woman more beautiful.'

Wonderful words to hear! If only he had loved her then words like those would have brought her running into his arms, to offer him her beauty, to let him see that it was his for the taking.

'And if I weren't beautiful?' she challenged, looking at him.

'Why ask a question like that? You are beautiful— and I want you.'

'One day,' she murmured, 'you might fall in love, and then you'll regret all these frivolous affairs you have.'

'They're not always frivolous. Admittedly there have been some I've regretted; it's inevitable. But I'd never regret having an affair with you, Jennifer. As for falling in love——' He laughed just as if the idea were non-sensical. 'Woman's stuff! In Greece we never fall in love!'

'I can't believe that.'

'Because you're English, and English girls are warm and sentimental.'

Her lashes came down again as she said,

'You've had affairs with English girls, then?'

'A few,' he admitted carelessly.

'Have you regretted any of them?'

He made no answer and she looked up, wondering if he had not heard her.

'What the devil is this?' he demanded, but with an edge of humour to his accented voice. 'A cross-examination conducted with a view to gaining knowledge of my morals before you commit yourself?'

She had to laugh, and noticed that his expression changed on the instant, and deep admiration filled his eyes.

'I admit I was curious about the affairs you'd had with my countrywomen, but as for my wanting to gain a knowledge of your morals before I commit myself— well, Luke, you don't seem to have understood me. I do not intend committing myself. I meant it when I said just now that I'm leaving your house today.'

'Scared—of me or of yourself?'

She drew a breath.

'You have the most inflated opinion of your attractions!'

'It's not so much that,' he returned, deliberately teasing her, 'as confidence in my powers of persuasion.'

'You're absurd,' she cried, quite unable to imagine his being like this with Elspeth. 'Your powers of persuasion leave me cold,' she decided to add, even though it was a long way from the truth. In fact, she was under no illusions as to her own weakness should he continue to tempt her. His very confidence was disconcerting in itself, and persuasive, and she strongly suspected he was well aware of it.

'They won't always leave you cold,' he asserted. 'There's something in you that hasn't yet been awakened——'

'I've finished my breakfast,' she interrupted, deciding to bring this conversation to an end before it became really intimate. 'I'd like to go and find out about several passengers I made friends with, and also to see if I can rescue any of my belongings from the ship.'

'I'll come with you,' he said decisively, and she gave a start. If he came with her, and she met people she had got to know on the ship, they would greet her as Colette. Yes, she mused, there were at least half a dozen people who would call her that—her table companions for one thing, because from the first they had used only Christian names.

'I'd rather go alone, if you don't mind.'

'Why? You'd be better with me around to assist. I'm quite useful, and in any case, if you do get your clothes you'll need a car to put them in.'

'I've got to find accommodation first.'

'You're staying here.' Imperious the voice, and challenging. Had anyone ever opposed his will? she wondered, fully aware that it would be much easier for her if she did not oppose it, for she was doubtful if she would be able to find accommodation, the island being so small, with only one hotel, Luke had said. .

She did manage to leave the house without him, but only because he was called to the telephone and from what Androula said, he was talking business and would be engaged for some considerable time.

'Mr Lucius haf long long talks with Athens man, you know, because he sells many tobaccos and fruits to Athens man who sells to shops and hotels. Mr Lucius grow manys of these things, and grapes for wine.'

Colette went down to the harbour to find many people milling about. She was just wondering what to do first when she was touched on the shoulder and turned to see the man who had talked to her in the boat, Luke's cousin.

'I thought it was you,' he smiled, 'but I wasn't sure. What a difference! You look very charming, if I may say so! No wonder Luke chose you to take home! Just like him——' He pulled himself up, grinning ruefully. Colette looked at him, examining his features to find some resemblance to his cousin, and found none. He was shorter, more swarthy of skin, and his hair was brown, not black, his mouth less severe and his eyes less hard. They were laughing as they looked into hers, but his voice was serious as he asked about the ordeal.

'You were burned, you said——'

'No, it was nothing,' she denied swiftly. 'Just my clothes that were scorched, nothing more.'

'You must have had a narrow escape, then?'

She shuddered, remaining silent, her searching glance having picked out several people she had chatted with on the ship.

'I've been helping an old lady who's travelling on her own,' he told her. 'She's managed to get some of her clothes and I've taken them to the hotel for her.'

'Is there any room left in the hotel?' she asked, and he looked at her in surprise.

'Aren't you comfortable where you are?'

'Oh—er—yes, but—but I'd rather be in the hotel.'

He looked at her searchingly, causing her colour to rise.

'Don't tell me he's made a pass at you already?' He threw back his head and laughed. 'He's incorrigible! No, I'm afraid there isn't anything for you at the hotel; they're bursting at the seams—up to half a dozen people sharing one room and half of them sleeping on the floor. Are you hoping to get some of your things off the ship?' he asked, changing the subject, his glance going to the small boat that was just pulling out, its object the liner anchored out from the shore. Colette could see now that its funnels were brown and that one end of the deck on which the ballroom was situated was nothing but a black mass of burnt timber and twisted metal.

'I *had* hoped to get some of my clothes,' she told him. 'Are they allowing passengers on board?'

'Yes, but you'll have to go into that shed over there first, and have your name and other particulars taken by the Purser's people.' He looked at her appraisingly, and asked her her name.

'Mrs Maddox,' she replied, and he grimaced.

'Your first name? We don't bother with surnames here—at least, not much.'

'Jennifer,' she said briefly.

'Mine's Petros. I don't live here all the time; I'm at university in Athens, but I'm on vacation for the next couple of months. My parents are retired here——' He pointed to a white villa high on a hill. 'That's their place. Come up if you like, and meet them.'

She thanked him and said yes, she would do that some time, but for the present she was concerned about her clothes, and especially her money and jewellery. She wanted him to leave her, for she was afraid of someone coming up to her and addressing her as Colette.

To her consternation he had no intention of leaving her, offering his assistance to get her to the ship if she was allowed to board.

'Come on,' he advised, 'and we'll get you registered— if that's what they call it.'

She had no alternative other than to let him accompany her. She saw a couple she had spoken to, but to them she had been Mrs Maddox from the start, as in fact she had been with most of the passengers. She was by nature reserved, and her life over the past eight years, both during her marriage and since, had been quietly spent in her home, with little opportunity to mix, and the result was that she found it difficult to adopt the friendly, spontaneous attitude which had seemed so prevalent with most of the people she met on her recent travels.

The couple smiled and stopped.

'Hello, Mrs Maddox. So you're safe. We knew you'd been trapped—one of the crew told us he'd broken a window for you to get out. How long are we to be here, do you think? We both have jobs and want to get back as soon as possible.'

They passed on, stopping to talk to someone else. At the Purser's improvised office in the shed on the harbour Colette was told she could go aboard on the launch provided, and she would be allowed to get her clothes if it was considered safe for her to enter her cabin.

'There is some danger of ceilings collapsing,' she was told. 'However, you will be accompanied by a member of crew, who will first examine your cabin. His advice will be taken. There will be no argument.'

'No. I understand. And my money?'

'Everything has been brought here from the Purser's office,' she was informed. She was questioned carefully before, having convinced the man that she really had deposited money and jewellery in the safe, she was asked to describe the jewellery. All this time Petros was outside, so he did not see her sign her name, Colette Maddox, when she was given the large envelope in which her valuables had been sealed. Nor could Petros accompany her on the launch. Everything was being done in a brisk, efficient way and no unauthorised person was allowed on the ship.

To Colette's delight she was able to rescue most of her clothes, only those in the wardrobe by the cabin door having been damaged, partly by fire and partly by water. Both her suitcases were unharmed, so she was able to push everything into them.

She questioned the crew member who was with her about obtaining accommodation.

'I'm in a private house at present,' she went on, 'but I'd like to go somewhere else.'

'That won't be possible. There isn't any accommodation to spare on the entire island. Everyone has taken someone in. Aren't you comfortable there?'

'Yes,' she had to admit, 'very comfortable.'

'Well then——?' He looked nonplussed and she allowed the matter to drop.

Petros was standing there when the launch returned.

He took the suitcases from the member of crew and carried them to a car.

'Jump in,' he invited, 'and I'll take you to Luke's. Oh, by the way, he'd told them in the Purser's place that he had a Mrs Maddox staying with him—told them late last night. Thinks of everything. They were glad to have the information because they'd listed you as missing.'

'It's kind of you to go to all this trouble,' she said. 'Is this your car?'

'No, my father's. I've just been doing some running about for a few other people.'

'How many people have your parents taken in?'

'Five—and I'm relegated to the verandah! It's a good thing it's summer, and that I like sleeping outside anyway!'

Luke was nowhere about when they arrived at his villa, which was less than five minutes' drive from the harbour. Set on a low hill among tall pines and with an olive grove to the north, it had a panoramic view to the sea and to the harbour, which was also the town. The vast and beautiful bay was completely sheltered from the northerly *meltemi* by the rising hills behind it. The little town, untarnished by tourists' shops and stalls, was a cluster of whitewashed, red-roofed villas occupying two hills which swept right down to the harbour. There were cafés with gay awnings, shops which faced the quay, where little *caiques* and luxury yachts were moored side by side in the dazzlingly clear, aquamarine waters of the Aegean. At one end of the harbour was a rocky island which could be approached by a causeway, and on this island could be seen three villas, all owned, said Petros, by millionaire friends of his cousin.

'Stella Logara lives there with her father,' he added

with an odd inflection in his voice. 'She's a dazzling beauty and the girl whom Luke will probably marry one day.'

'Marry ...?' A sudden hollowness within her caused her voice to fail momentarily. 'He—he's going to marry, then?'

They were on the verandah outside the sitting-room, Petros having taken her suitcases from the car and put them in the hall. He glanced at her strangely as she spoke, as though something in her tone had caught and held his attention.

'He'll marry—yes, of course. All men must marry one day.'

'But he seems the kind of man who'll—er—have a good time all his life.'

Petros gave a crack of laughter.

'He *will* have a good time all his life. Stella's ambitious; she's not interested in very much besides money, so she'll not mind if Luke has his pillow-friends.'

'You believe he'll be unfaithful to his wife?'

'All Greek men are unfaithful to their wives,' he replied casually. 'We are not like your cold Englishmen, you know.' He stopped and listened. 'I can hear Luke's car. He's just turning into the drive.'

His car swept into view from a curve of palm trees, then slid smoothly and almost silently to a halt. Luke leapt out, his sparse, upright frame buoyant with health, his black eyes smiling as they rested on Colette's face.

'You should have waited for me,' he admonished. 'How have you gone on? I see you enlisted the aid of this young tearaway!'

'Petros has been a great help,' she returned. 'I've got most of my clothes and all my money and jewellery.'

'Fine. I've been hearing that everyone's accounted

for, and safe. There are a few injured in the hospital, and a few more who are out-patients, but nothing serious at all.'

'It's certainly caused some excitement on Attikon,' said Petros. 'We're on the map at last!'

'Where are your clothes?' Luke wanted to know, glancing at Colette. 'Has someone taken them up to your room for you?' His black eyes flickered over her face admiringly. Petros, watching him, said banteringly,

'Jennifer wanted to find fresh lodgings, so I wondered if you'd been making a pass at her. She's not used to your kind, Luke, you can see that, surely?'

Luke turned to him, his gaze narrowed.

'You talk out of turn, Petros, as usual. Off you go. We're obliged for your help, but you've outstayed your welcome. Remember me to Aunt Maria and Uncle Stephanos.'

'I will. You're as unsociable as ever—to *me*,' Petros added with a significant glance at Colette.

'I must thank you again,' put in Colette, smiling. 'I'll remember your invitation and come over to see your parents.'

'They'll make you welcome. How about coming to dinner this evening? You'll be with others from the ship.'

'Jennifer's dining here, with me,' stated Luke with quiet authority. 'Goodbye, Petros.'

'But why should you have all the luck——?'

'*Tha hasso tin ipomomi moo!*'

'It's bad manners to talk Greek when your guest can't understand.'

Luke's eyes glinted.

'I've just warned you, Petros ... I shall lose my patience!'

'Oh, all right! But she's not your prisoner, you know! She can come and see us whenever she likes.' Petros turned away, ran down the steps and got into his car. He grinned good-humouredly at them both as he drove off, turning from the forecourt into the drive.

'So you wanted to leave me?' Luke's voice was smooth and soft. 'What excuse did you give him?'

'None.'

'If I know my cousin he'd want some explanation.'

'He found one for himself,' Colette said. 'He took it for granted that you'd made a pass at me—you just heard what he said.'

'Did you deny it?'

'The subject was changed.'

'Most convenient.' He looked at her mockingly. 'Would you have denied it, Jennifer?'

'I'd have been evasive.'

'And you're being evasive now.'

She gave an audible sigh.

'I think I shall go and change. I ought to be returning Androula's clothes to her.' She moved away, slowly, almost reluctantly. For he drew her, this dark Greek with the pagan face and arrogant manner that would have done credit to the god Zeus himself.

She heard his command as she reached the open french window through which she intended to enter the house.

'Jennifer . . . come here.'

She swung round, a wild throbbing in her heart.

'Yes—wh-what is it?'

He pointed to a spot by his feet.

'Here,' he murmured, and again she moved, as if impelled by some magnetic force against which her puny resistance would have no effect whatsoever.

'Yes,' she said again in a husky whisper. 'What is it, Luke?'

'I heard today that a ship will be here on Friday to take the passengers on board. It's expected that the cruise will be resumed.'

She was close, looking up into his face, a formidable face, unsmiling and almost harsh.

'On Friday,' she repeated, turbulence within her, and a spate of doubt and indecision. 'That's—that's the day after tomorrow.' It seemed as if she were speaking of the day of doom, and yet, only a few hours ago, she was telling Petros that she wanted to leave here.

'Yes, Jennifer, the day after tomorrow.' He looked down at her, into soft, limpid eyes, then lower to the full, sensitive mouth that twisted into a smile of constraint.

'We'll b-be saying—saying goodbye, then—er—quite soon.'

He took her chin in his hand.

'You're not going,' he told her implacably. 'You're staying here, with me.'

'Don't be silly!' she said, and twisted away.

Luke shook his head in a gesture of admonishment.

'You know as well as I that we can't say goodbye—not yet. Not for a long time, in fact. Write to your housekeeper and tell her where you are and that you'll be here for some months, even longer. Tell her you've found an island which you like and you've rented a house—— Tell her anything you like; it doesn't matter.'

The turbulence remained ... but the doubts were fading....

'If I stay ... where will I live?'

'Here, of course.'

'As your—pillow-friend, I think your cousin termed that particular kind of woman.'

His mouth went tight.

'I said that Petros speaks out of turn!'

'I would be your pillow-friend, though?'

'We'd be lovers, yes.'

She said, marvelling at the steadiness of her voice when she was so near to tears,

'Do you usually have your pillow-friends living here?'

'I've never had one living here before. You'll be the first,' he added with a smile.

'Your aunt and uncle—they live close. Don't you care that they'd know?'

'What has my life or morals to do with them?' he demanded, sudden arrogance in his tone.

'Greeks baffle me,' was all she could find to say.

'We're honest. We hide nothing.'.

'Petros was saying that you would probably marry one day.'

'It isn't beyond the bounds of possibility——' Luke stopped, his eyes narrowing. 'What else did he say?'

'He told me about someone called Stella,' she answered, and heard him give a smothered exclamation of anger.

'He wants a rap over the knuckles!'

Colette looked at him for a long moment before saying,

'Has this Stella ever been your pillow-friend?'

'If she had,' replied Luke slowly, 'then there would be no question of her ever becoming my wife.'

'Because Greeks never marry their mistresses.' She was recalling words uttered years ago by Meriel.

'That is correct.'

She nodded slowly, still looking up at him.

'You wouldn't care that this Stella—and her father —would know you had me for—for your——'

'Greek women understand these things,' he broke in, saving her further difficulty. 'She might be jealous, but it would be nothing. She would probably give me the cold shoulder for a while, but she'd come round, once you and I had parted.'

So casual about it all! Colette's heart was crying. She had weakened for a few moments, half believing that she could make him love her, that by giving herself to him, body and soul, and with all the love that was in her, she would sow some small seed that would grow and flourish into a love as strong as her own.

It was not to be, because by his own admission he would never marry a woman he had had as his mistress.

She spoke at last, to say simply, a sob in her voice that she hoped he would not hear,

'I can't stay with you, Luke. It's an absurd idea, you must know that.'

He stared, stepping back as if he had received a blow.

'What made you change your mind?' he demanded harshly. 'You'd practically decided to stay. You asked me where you would live——' He glowered at her. 'You can't change your mind! You're as much drawn to me as I to you! It's fate——'

'Luke,' she broke in gently, 'there's no argument as far as I'm concerned. I admit I had weakened, but it was only fleetingly. I'm not that kind of woman, Luke,' she went on earnestly. 'Perhaps I'm old fashioned, but I couldn't have a sordid affair like that with a man, just for the pleasure of the moment.'

'Sordid!' he exclaimed. 'You believe it would be sordid?'

'Wouldn't it, when we were intending to part—in a few months, I think you said?'

He drew an exasperated breath.

'I can't let you go, Jennifer! I want you as I've never wanted a woman in my life—and I shall have you!'

She turned away, blinking rapidly to hold back the tears. She had not taken more than a couple of steps when her wrist was seized and she was brutally swung around, her body brought against his, and before she had time even to utter the protest that leapt to her lips they were savagely crushed beneath his hard and merciless mouth. She struggled, but in vain, twisting her head and escaping his lips, but only for a second before hers were captured again and forced open, while his hand came round to hold her breast within the insistent grip of his fingers.

'Oh . . .' she quivered when at last he relaxed his hold upon her, 'let me go! I—I hate you!' The tears welled up, flooded her eyes then fell on to her cheeks. 'You're a brute!' she cried, her whole body shaking with emotion awakened in a way she had never known before. If this was desire—real desire born of love—then she had missed more than she ever realised, for despite her anger, and Luke's unbridled passion that almost frightened her, she could have surrendered . . . so very easily.

'You don't hate me,' he was stating softly. 'You want me as much as I want you, Jennifer, and you'll stay with me. I was never so sure of anything in the whole of my life.'

CHAPTER SEVEN

COLETTE stood on the talcum-soft sand and stared out to where the crippled ship lay at anchor. She had come from Luke's villa, to wander alone on to the beach. Her mind was confused still, but she had been able to make a firm resolve, which was to leave Attikon with the other cruise passengers in two days' time. Luke could not keep her here—unless of course he decided to make her a prisoner. But even were he to go to that extreme he dared not assault her, force his attentions on her against her will. She knew he would never do that in any case.

What he was fully expecting was for her to be unable to resist him, and this proved that always in his dealings with women he had found himself to be irresistible. He was a proud and pompous man, but she had known this a long time ago, had admitted that he was not a *nice* man, not in the way that Davy was nice. Davy was gentle and kind, unassuming and on occasions a little unsure of himself. Luke on the other hand rode roughshod over the women he preyed upon; he was egotistical, too full of his own importance and conscious of his good looks, his perfect physique, his ability to bring women to his feet. Elspeth was a fair example; she had succumbed to his charms, had wanted him, desperately, cherishing the hope that he meant marriage. He must have been sneering at her, taking all she gave with not the slightest degree of guilt or contrition on that night when he bade her goodbye.

Colette wondered just how many women he had

treated in this way. Dozens, probably, so how could she have been so optimistic as to hope that she would be his last love? No, he was only in his thirties; he had a long way to go yet before he met his last love. It was doubtful if he would ever meet her. He was half resigned to marrying Stella Logara, whom he obviously did not even have affection for, much less any deeper feeling.

A sigh escaped her as her gaze became once more focused on the ship. If only the other ship would come now, instead of Friday! If only she could get away, and begin to forget all over again. She should not have come on these travels; this would never have happened had she stayed at home. Home ... where she was safe from the world's hurts and from men like Luke Marlis, the man whose image had haunted her for years.

The slow chugging of *caiques* and the more aggressive engines of speeding power boats filtered the silence and she turned towards the harbour, at the very end of the wide crescent. Stately yachts swayed gently in the breeze, their sails white or red, billowing slightly. Fishermen mending nets, another slapping a freshly-caught octopus on the hard ground, tenderising it. Silver olive groves rising from the shore, and beyond them the dark pinewoods, mysterious, perhaps concealing remains of ancient temples where pagan gods were worshipped. The island for Colette could have spelled enchantment; it drew her irresistibly ... but she must not stay.

A sound behind her brought her head around. Petros, smiling with those happy eyes of his, a dog at his heels.

'Hello, there! *Yassoo!* I greet you!'

She laughed, finding it good to have his company if only for a short spell.

'Hello, Petros. Is this your dog?' She bent to pat him, a long-eared, long-tailed mongrel with a shaggy coat.

'I brought him back from Athens last summer. There are many strays in that city. He was starving, poor thing.'

'You have a kind heart,' she said, straightening up and brushing the hair out of her eyes. 'Did you know that a new ship's arriving on Friday to take us all off here?'

'No.' He frowned at her. 'What a shame. I had hoped we'd have you for a bit—at least a week. Gosh, are the Greeks bucking up their ideas? It's usually *avrio* or *siga, siga!*'

'What does that mean?'

'*Avrio* means tomorrow—any old day. *Siga, siga* is slowly, slowly—don't hurry yourself; you've all the time in the world! That's why we all look so young! We never worry our heads about what might happen next year, or even next week.'

'How old are you?' she asked, and was told he was twenty-three.

'Luke considers me a babe still in the nursery. I shall be a mere forty when he's fifty-three, and serve him right!'

'It'll be a long long time before he's fifty-three,' she said, thinking that he would never look old, not with features like those.

'He won't be liking the idea of your going away so soon. I saw the way he looked at you—watch him, Jennifer. He's a rake! He's broken more hearts than he himself can count.'

'That must be an exaggeration,' she returned with an unconscious touch of anger.

'Who told you about the new ship?'

'Luke did.'

'Was he all right about it? I mean, didn't he ask you to stay, or anything?'

She cast him a curious glance.

'What makes you say that, Petros?'

'The way he looks at you.' He wagged a playful finger at her. 'I happen to know that look, Jennifer. I means he'd like to go to bed with you——'

'Petros—please!' she broke in, flashing him a furious glance. 'It was no such thing!'

His eyes widened with perception as the colour began to fuse her cheeks at the memory of the scene which had taken place just an hour or so ago.

'He *has* made a pass at you! How could I have doubted it? A beautiful girl there for rescuing—— Didn't I say it was easy to see why he'd given you hospitality and not the two others he'd rescued? They could go elsewhere, but you were the star prize——'

'He wouldn't know what I looked like, not in the state I was in!' she flashed.

Petros slanted an eyebrow.

'My dear girl, Luke can spot them in any circumstances. He's been leading a dull life—for him—in recent months, just staying quietly here. So you're providing a diversion—a much-needed one,' he added with a sort of amused significance which brought even more colour to her face. 'A widow in any case is always easy game—a young widow, that is.' He glanced at her finger and added curiously, 'You're young to be widowed, but he told me you were. *Are* you a widow, or was it a divorce? Or perhaps you have a husband, all unsuspecting, at home?'

She glared at him.

'I have no husband! And I don't know what you mean by "unsuspecting".'

He merely shrugged and said,

'I'm sorry, Jennifer. It was just that some women take a holiday on their own for no other purpose than to have a bit of fun with someone else for a week or so.'

'I think,' she decided coldly, 'we'll change the subject——'

'Why?' came a voice from a small copse to the side of where they were standing. 'Is this pup annoying you?'

'Luke!' Petros glowered at him. 'Why the devil do you always appear at the wrong time!'

Luke flicked him an indifferent glance before turning his full attention on Colette.

'You're blushing, Jennifer. Has he been insulting you?'

She turned away and began to walk along the beach. Luke soon caught her up, as she knew he would. His appearance had affected her as much as ever, and her heart was beating far too quickly as she sent him an upward glance.

'He was embarrassing you, I believe,' said Luke harshly. 'Why did you stay and listen?'

'He told you what he'd been saying?' she asked in surprise.

'I got some of it out of him,' replied Luke tautly. 'Why didn't you walk away?'

'I suppose I thought it would be rude,' she answered without much interest. 'It doesn't matter. I shall be leaving here within forty-eight hours.'

Leaving. . . . After being with Luke, after having his entire interest, awakening in him a desire which, when she was a mere child of seventeen, would have sent her soaring to the skies.

'You won't leave.' Luke's quiet, accented voice was both confident and uncompromising. 'There is too much for you here.' He had paced ahead unconsciously,

but slowed his step immediately, to suit hers. Colett
stared out to sea—so calm it was, and blue. She felt tha
it should be lashing itself into a fury of foam-creste
waves; it would have suited her condition better. Fc
she was in a turmoil of indecision again. It would b
wonderful to stay, and taste the love she had craved i
those far-off days ... the love she had missed in th
unproductive years of her sacrificial marriage. She wa
almost twenty-five and had not yet tasted the ecstasy c
love. ... But would she taste the ecstasy of love if sh
stayed with him?

On Luke's side there was no love and never woul
be, no question of marriage because he would neve
marry a woman who had given herself to him already
What an old-fashioned idea in these permissive times
But then this was the East, where change was slow
where man was the master, reigning supreme over th
women of his household. Yet Luke had travelled ex
tensively in the West; he must know of the equality c
the sexes, of the fact that no longer was a woma
stigmatised for doing those things which for a ma
were accepted as part of the necessities of his life. H
spoke excellent English, had influential friends ove
there, in her country. ... Yes, he ought to have bee
more understanding and allowed that a woman was no
tainted simply because—— She cut her reverie, awar
that it was just a waste of time simply because Luke di
not seem to be capable of deep, sincere love. So wha
difference would it make if he did excuse her be
haviour? He still would not marry her.

'My dear,' he murmured, 'you're very quiet. Wha
are you thinking?' He was smiling faintly, lookin
down at her with those piercing black eyes. 'Ho
tantalising you are,' he went on before she could speak
'Do you really expect me to let such a prize escape m

before I've had the opportunity to enjoy it?'

'Petros referred to me as the star prize,' she mused. 'I'm afraid, Luke, you'll have to look around for another. I expect they're there for the picking up——'

'Be quiet!' he broke in wrathfully. 'As for Petros— if I'd had any idea he'd be about I'd not have allowed you out!'

'What?' She blinked at him, her chin lifting. 'Do you realise what you said?'

He sighed impatiently.

'Do you want me to apologise for kissing you?' he asked, changing the subject.

'An apology wouldn't do much good.'

'You seem exceedingly calm about it all.'

'I wasn't at the time. The peace round here——' She swung a hand, and her body at the same time. 'It does things to your nerves—calms them.'

Luke stopped, taking her hand in a gentle grasp.

'You're a strange girl, Jennifer—mysterious, ethereal. I'm fascinated by you, by the quietness which I know hides something that I'd like to discover—— Why have you started like that?' he suddenly asked in surprise. 'What did I say to make you nervous?'

'Nothing—nothing at all.' She tried to withdraw her hand, but his grip on it tightened.

'Something I'd like to discover....' he repeated thoughtfully. 'Yes, that was what made you nervous.' He stood above her, toweringly magnificent, his eyes searching, disconcerting her just as his words had done. How had he come to guess that she had a secret? The man was omniscient! However, he had no idea what her secret could be and his puzzlement could not embarrass her. 'I haven't ever met anyone remotely like you,' he went on. 'Women I have met have always been so transparent——' There was a sneer of contempt in the tone of voice he used, and in his eyes a hint of sardonic amusement. 'Never have I been intrigued by a woman; the experience is new ... and challenging, my dear. I shall not let you go.'

'You can't stop me,' she returned gently. 'I shall be collected like the rest of the passengers and taken aboard the new ship.'

'And I am to stand on the shore and watch you sail away?' Slowly spoken words carrying derision. 'No, Jennifer! That sort of submission is not in my line at all. What I want I get, and what I have I hold.' He glanced down at her hand in his; he opened his palm and a strange unfathomable smile hovered on his lips. 'Pretty ... dainty. But it is you——' His eyes lifted to settle on her lovely face, which was pale, with her mouth moving spasmodically, result of the chaos within her. Should she stay? No, it would hurt too much when he tired of her and cast her off! But the intervening time? It would be bliss.... It was *more* than chaos; her mind was a labyrinth of tangled thoughts, desire battling with wisdom, stumbling inconsistency with firm decision. 'Jennifer,' he murmured, bending his head to touch her lips with his own, 'stay with me. Give me your promise now, this moment. I know you'd never break it.'

She shook her head, tears sparkling on her lashes.

'I can't!' she cried desperately. 'Leave me alone! I'm not like that—it's against my principles——'

'You want to stay,' he interrupted her quietly. 'Follow your natural inclinations, child, and put these ideals behind you.'

'No,' she said, and now, by some miracle, her brain was clear. From the disorder one word had emerged: heartache. It was before her eyes, in glaring capitals. It would be heartache for the rest of her life if she followed her natural inclinations, as he termed it. 'I've definitely made up my mind. I'm going home.'

She saw his mouth tighten, wondered if ever in his experience with women he had been thwarted as he was now. He had been so confident of his power to entice, his magnetism as a drawing force. Well, for once things had not gone his way.

'What makes you so stubborn, child?' It was several hours later that the question was put to Colette. She and Luke were on the patio at sunset, both having changed for dinner, she into a halter-necked gown which closed around her firm young breasts as if it had been moulded there, the honey-lustre of her skin contrasting with the pure white satin of which the dress was made. The waist clung, with copious folds flaring out to form a wide hemline trimmed with lace-edged flouncing. It was a Paris model bought for the cruise, while she was in Genoa; Luke's eyes had widened to their full extent when he saw her appear in it, coming down the wide staircase with all the regal distinction of a queen. He, in pearl-grey linen with a frilled mauve evening shirt beneath the jacket, had been standing in the hall staring at a huge bowl of oleanders which Katrina, his buxom, middle-aged housekeeper, had picked that day from along the stream and put into the vase. Colette's descent had attracted his attention and he had turned, swinging his long lithe body without moving his feet, and she sensed that he had caught his breath, that a new emotion had spread like some uncontrollable distributary through his entire mind and body. The moment was tense, electrically charged, and she had halted her steps part way down the stairs, to flutter a smile at him, while the spell remained, affecting them both.

'My God, Jennifer, you look adorable....' Quietly-spoken words which broke the spell, reverent words, almost. His eyes were sweeping over her, up and down and up again to fix themselves on her face. 'That dress, and you—what a combination!'

She had smiled again, thinly this time, bleakly aware that he saw her only as an object of desire, burning, pagan desire that her surrender alone could satisfy.

They had come out to the patio for an aperitif, as dinner was never served before half-past eight.

'What makes me so stubborn?' she repeated, holding her glass against the rosy globe that protected the candle from the flutter of a breeze coming in from the sea. 'You consider me to be stubborn just because I won't be your pillow-friend?' She was calm, with no indecision about her now. How long before some word of his, some glance or smile, brought disorder to her mind again she did not know. For the present she was bidding her subconscious mind to help and guide her, to shield her in an armour of determination and purpose.

'Perhaps I ought not to have used the word,' he admitted unexpectedly. 'Reluctance would be a better. Why are you reluctant to stay with me?'

Something made her laugh; perhaps she was a trifle hysterical, she thought, harassed as she was by his unflagging persistence.

'Why do you bother, Luke? Is it pique at not getting all your own way? Or is it a sense of failure which you can't bear to experience?'

'It is certainly not a joke,' he told her harshly, 'as you appear to suppose it is!'

'I'm sorry; I don't know why I laughed.' She sipped her sherry, then lowered the glass slowly on to the table, letting the crimson glow on the amber liquid create

colours similar to those being created by the blood-red
sun suspended over the horizon.

Luke changed the subject, asking her to tell him
about her home in England.

'You've told me it's in Devon,' he went on, 'and that
you have a large estate and a big house. But what is it
like? I'm interested to know.' His eyes lingered for a
moment on the beautiful necklace she was wearing,
with eardrops and a bracelet to match. The set, of flaw-
less diamonds, was an extra to the jewellery given her
by Uncle Patrick, and had been found in another safe,
behind the wardrobe in his bedroom.

She began to talk, her voice low and solemn; she was
guarded, as there was much to conceal. Her face
clouded as she told him about the car, which had been
the old man's treasure, and it was fated to be the cause
of her mother's death and that of her husband.

'And you weren't in the car, you say?' He opened his
eyes wide, as if compelling her to look full into them.
But she avoided doing so, lowering her lashes, all unaware that they sent shadows on to her cheeks which
her companion found to be inordinately delectable.

'No,' she murmured, 'I was not in the car.'

'It must have been a terrible shock to you.'

'Of course. I was a long time getting over it.'

'And you would be only about twenty-two when you
found yourself with a large estate to manage?'

'I was not yet twenty-two. I had excellent workers on
the farm, one of whom took over all the responsibility
while I was in —— While I was so—upset.'

Luke's eyes narrowed again; he reached for his glass
and put it to his lips, regarding her with an unfathomable expression over the rim of it.

'You haven't mentioned how you met your husband,'
he murmured, tilting the glass to take a drink.

She looked at him, a frown creasing her brow.

'Why this interest? We're merely acquaintances. You haven't told me anything about yourself,' she reminded him, 'so why should I give you a résumé of my past history?' He made no answer for the moment and she went on to add, 'You and I, Luke, are merely ships that pass in the night. Within less than forty-eight hours we shall have said goodbye, never to meet again.'

'You've said that once—or something like it,' he almost snapped. 'I shan't argue with you any more, but——' he lifted his other hand to wag a forefinger at her, 'I know what I know ... and what I want. You shall not leave here on Friday; I can promise you that.'

Colette glanced away impatiently, watching the sunset, fascinated by the way its fiery glow painted the water and sent a molten stream of ripples to the shore, where they died, only to be followed by more.

In Greece the sun's descent was swift, and even as she watched, the great sphere was rapidly disappearing, taking most of the fire with it but leaving glorious hues of bronze and saffron and pure burnished gold. On the breeze came the elusive drift of perfume from a lemon grove in Luke's grounds; it mingled with the wafting scent of roses to create a fragrance as heady as it was indescribable.

And over all was that eternal silence found only on an island ... an unspoilt island like Attikon where the old Greek way of life still prevailed, and where the only sign of modernisation was the few villas belonging to the wealthy Greeks who had built them, and two small hotels.

Luke spoke again, this time to make another change of subject.

'You said just now that I hadn't told you anything about myself. What is it you want to know?'

'It's not important, Luke,' she said, and knew her indifference annoyed him.

'It's natural that you'd be curious,' he stated. 'Where would you like me to begin?'

She had to smile.

'Is there anything to tell besides your escapades with my sex? From what I can gather your life's been one long series of affairs.'

'So the angel has claws,' he murmured with a smile. 'I'd not have suspected it. You're so gentle, you see— though provocative and tantalising.' He paused, watching her take up her glass, lifting it to her lips. 'I do have business affairs to see to. And in addition I have other interests.'

'Such as?'

His eyes glinted.

'Jennifer,' he said in a very soft tone that made her nerves tingle even before the next words were uttered, 'I advise you not to adopt that sceptical manner with me. A young relative did so once, to her cost, and I gave her the spanking of her life.'

Colette went fiery red.

'You wouldn't dare lay a finger on me!' she shot at him. 'You're far too familiar! We haven't known one another any time at all....' Her voice trailed, because she was remembering that she had known him for a long time, even though they'd been far apart, had known him, and loved him ... and wanted him, as she wanted him at this moment. She would not trust herself, she thought, if he were to take her in his arms again, and crush her body and her lips to his.

'I feel I've known you for years,' he said slowly, thoughtfully, an odd expression in his eyes. 'I'm baffled....' It was to himself he spoke now, so softly that she had to strain her ears to catch the words. 'Baffled

by ... I don't know what....' He looked at her and
added curiously, 'Has it not struck you that you yourself are familiar? Take the way you've called me
Luke——'

'You told me that was your name,' she cut in, startled.
'What do you mean, I'm familiar?'

'It's the *way* you say my name. You were never shy
about it, and yet you're a shy girl, aren't you?'

'Not particularly shy,' she denied, her nerves alert as
a wave of apprehension swept over her. Was it possible
that he could guess who she was? She had had the impression once or twice that he was listening carefully to
her voice, as if something in its modulation had caught
his attention. Or could it be that a faint, elusive thread
of memory was troubling him? He was right, of course,
when he maintained that she had used his name with
ease, and only now did she realise that, if he *had* been
a total stranger, she would have taken time to get to
the point of using his Christian name, because she *was*
of a shy nature, just as he had obviously discovered.

She watched him as he maintained a thoughtful
silence, and adroitly attempted to change his train of
thought by commenting on the glory of the sunset.

'Just look at the colours,' she added, pointing. 'The
sky was copper a few moments ago, but now it's pink
and peach and lovely shades of mauve.'

The black eyes flickered perceptively. He said with a
trace of satire,

'You baffle me more when you try to be clever.' He
obligingly looked across the sea. 'You are right; the sky
has changed colour in the last few minutes, but it
always does, very quickly, in this part of the world, as
you must know.' Even as he spoke the colours began to
blend with each other until, in the dusky twilight, the
shore became a nebulous monochrome of shadows,

mysterious and beautiful in the fleeting interlude that awaits the fall of night.

'The ship looks forlorn,' she said, and heard a light laugh escape him. She thought—as she had thought so many times in the few short hours since she had come to his island—that he had never been like this with Elspeth, never been so relaxed and free, so quick to smile and laugh. In fact, come to think of it, she had never known him to laugh in those days. Her memory brought back only a formidable face and hard metallic eyes, a thin mouth, an implacable jaw. Arrogance and superiority were never absent; sarcasm had sometimes brought the colour flooding to Elspeth's face.

No, he had never been like this with her stepsister ... so why the change? Had the years mellowed him? Or was it she, Colette, who was awakening in him something that had been dormant up till now ...? Crazy, ambitious ideas! She thrust them away behind the knowledge that his only interest in her was her body.

'You can't think of anything to say, can you?' He laughed again, bringing a flush of colour to her cheeks. 'I'm charmed with you, Jennifer. You're provocatively stimulating. What is it about you that's so different from the other women I have known?'

'For one thing,' she retorted, 'I'm able to resist your overtures.'

'For how long?' He rose from his chair and she froze on the instant.

'Don't you touch me!' she cried, getting up from her own chair and moving warily away from him until her back touched a white marble support and she could go no further.

'Afraid, my love? I *shall* touch you ... and make you want *even more*.'

'No!' She was terribly afraid—afraid of herself and

of him, of the moonlight that now drenched the sea and the shore and the lovely gardens with luminous silver. 'Go away from me——'

He had her in his arms, bringing her to him with an ease that made her own strength and struggles laughable.

His hand came beneath her chin; she was forced to look into those black eyes, and she trembled at the fire in them. She was lost, she felt; she must be, for how could she resist him when she wanted him as much as he wanted her? His lips sought hers and she found herself reciprocating, allowing her lips to be forced apart, thrilling to the insistent exploration of his mouth. She could feel his hard and sinewed body moving rhythmically against the slender curves of her own, was vitally alive to the virility of him, the power of his touch as his long lean fingers explored with arrogant possessiveness the curve of her back before slowly sliding themselves underneath the bodice of her dress, to caress her breast in a way that sent her pulses racing, fanning to a flame of urgent desire the craving for the fulfilment of her love for him.

His passionate kisses, the mastery of his embrace, the touch of his hand ... all had the erotic stamp of pagan uncontrol, and she was borne like a leaf in the wind into the tempest of his ardour, and even when he made to pick her up she had no strength to protest, although she knew his intention was to carry her from the patio to a little arbour hidden by jacaranda trees and with bougainvillaea vines tumbling over its walls.

But no sooner had he begun to lift her than he drew away sharply, turning to the rail an instant before Davos appeared to say that dinner was served.

He waited until the man had gone and then laughed. 'So near and yet so far, my love,' he said with mocking amusement, his eyes on her flushed face, then moving to her heaving chest. 'And now, my Jennifer, are you going to keep up the pretence that you want to leave me?'

CHAPTER EIGHT

THE ship was out there, riding the waves. Colette, with her suitcases packed and already in the hall, was by the window in the sitting-room, her heart dead within her. She had managed to keep Luke's ardour at bay, while desperately hoping for the miracle that would bring her willingly to his side. She knew for sure that he found her attractive in a way he had never found a woman attractive before, and she felt that if only time were on her side she could win his lasting love. But the ship was there, and already many of the passengers had been taken aboard, transported by several launches that were plying back and forth between ship and shore.

She turned as Luke entered the room, his face black as thunder, his hands clenched at his sides.

'You are ready for me to take you to the harbour?'

She nodded, swallowing hard.

'Yes—thank you, Luke.'

He preserved an icy silence during the short journey, and while he was taking her luggage from the car.

'Thank you,' she said again, looking up at him, a wistful shadow in her big blue eyes. 'You've been—been very kind to—to me.'

He gritted his teeth, glowering at her.

'You're glad to be going, all the same,' he snapped.

'You *assume* that I'm glad to be going,' she corrected. 'Aren't you?'

She shrugged, feeling that another argument would only distress them both. There was still some hustle and bustle, with luggage and passengers being taken aboard the small boats.

'I'll say goodbye, Luke. I can see one of the crew coming to put my cases on the launch.'

He stared broodingly down at her, a nerve pulsating in his throat. He was furiously angry, having lost a battle he had been so arrogantly confident of winning. He could have beaten her into submission and she knew it. Never in the whole of his life had he been so frustrated.

'You needn't go yet. Take the last launch!' Imperious the tone, commanding. His eyes were on fire with challenge; he was daring her to argue with his decision. Pompous, hateful man! How could she love him?

She turned away from the harsh severity of his face, and marvelled at the peace she encountered. The high hills drowsy in the afternoon sun, their summits sharp-edged against a Grecian sky of sapphire blue; the carob slopes further down, and lower still the fields of lush green pasture with the silver ribbon of a stream meandering through a small, tree-sided valley. White villas on the plateau, the gleaming white campanile of a church rising from an olive grove beside a village, a woman tending a few goats; and another, all in black, leading a donkey laden with brushwood. The fresh lucid atmosphere, the quivering pulsation of light reflected on the sea ... and the ship out there, the ship that would take her away from this island paradise ... and from the man she would never see again.

A shuddering sigh escaped her. How could she say goodbye? Luke was hers if she only said the word ... hers for a few months of bliss.... And after that, to be cast off, told lightly that it was all finished. Yes, in that same callous manner in which he had said his last goodbye to her stepsister.

She thought of the dull routine of home, of the

burden of responsibility that awaited her, and she closed her eyes tightly, almost wishing she could die.

'I'd better go,' she said hollowly. 'There's nothing to be gained by my taking the last launch....' Her voice hung suspended as she saw him wave away the man who came to pick up her luggage.

'Later!' he said authoritatively. 'Mrs Maddox will go in the last launch.'

'Very good, sir.' The man went away to collect a suitcase that seemed to have been left behind by some-one. It was put on to the launch, which, after a few more people had boarded it, drew away, its engine throbbing against the pull of the tide.

The last launch was filling up. Colette moved from Luke's side, saying as she went towards the boat,

'Goodbye, Luke, and give my regards to Petros.'

'I will,' came his brief and cold reply.

And then she was on the launch, with her luggage being put in at the stern, along with some other suit-cases. People were waving to those who had put them up, shouting their thanks, promising to come back some time for a holiday. Colette sat looking down at the handbag on her knee, determined not to look up, or to wave to Luke. No use causing herself more pain by collecting a memory like that.

She boarded the ship and, following instructions she had already been given, went straight to the Purser's office and gave in her name, as everyone had to be accounted for.

It was all very smooth and trouble-free. The ship sailed before dark and the routine of the cruise was re-sumed, the next stop being the island of Skiros, an island famous in legend and history; Theseus had died there, and Achilles was there, too, hidden by the daughters of Lycodemus.

Colette determinedly attended the short lecture given before they landed, so that she would know a little about it. But her heart was not in it, or anything else for that matter. She wanted to get back home, throw herself into some work, and forget there ever was a man called Luke Marlis.

The ship stayed for nine hours and was due to sail at eight in the evening. Colette had been with a young couple for part of the time, but their company began to pall and, having made an excuse to get away, she walked along the waterfront on her own. She kept glancing at her watch, almost willing the time to pass.

And, just when she was about to make her way to the part of the harbour where the ship lay at anchor, she saw it—Luke's motor launch, the one into which she had been hauled by Petros after being rescued from the sea by his cousin. Luke! What was he doing here? Business? Or had she forgotten something—some of her jewellery? Dazed by the appearance of the boat, she found it impossible to think. The launch had been moored by his own private landing-stage when she came away; she remembered seeing it as they left the villa. Fascinated, she could not move, for her body was as inactive as her brain. The boat was speeding towards the harbour, passing yachts and fishing *caiques*, sending up a foamy white spray high into the air.

'No....' She shook her head as if the idea that had entered it was something to be got rid of swiftly. 'No, it can't be that.... He hasn't come to—to see—m-me....'

He had spotted her! His hand was raised in a salute; she saw the expression on his face; he was smiling as if he had suddenly scored some kind of a victory.

She swayed as, having tied up the launch, he leapt ashore and strode towards her. Why were her legs so weak, her nerves stretched to breaking point? Why was her throat blocked, her body shaking uncontrollably?

'Jennifer. . . .' He stopped, then came on again, gripping her by the shoulders so roughly that she flinched at the pain.

'Come back, dear. I won't molest you or tempt you. Just be my guest. Stay for a while. I can't let you go, and it suddenly dawned on me that if I asked you to stay as my guest you'd accept.' He held her more gently, his eyes soft, persuasive. 'You said something that made me realise that you didn't want to leave—remember, when you said I was *assuming* that you were glad to be going? Well, much as I want you in *that* way, Jennifer, I'm willing to have you just as a friend. You will come, dear? Say you'll have a holiday with me?'

Her heart was light as air! Time. . . . Obviously he had *some* feeling for her, as otherwise he would not have gone to all this trouble to get her back. And if only she had time. . . . But, suddenly suspicious and filled with doubts, she said, looking squarely at him,

'You mean it, Luke? You're sincere? I can trust you?'

He nodded his head.

'You can trust me, Jennifer. I've said I won't molest you and I mean it.'

Still she hesitated, aware of a little access of foreboding. But on looking again into his face she was partly reassured.

'There'll be difficulties, surely?'

Again the doubts, a fear in her heart that she was acting impulsively.

'There's nothing to stop you leaving the ship whenever you want to,' he smiled. 'I'll come back with you, of course, and we'll collect your things.'

'Yes—y-yes—all right, Luke.'

'What's wrong, dear?' He looked at her anxiously. 'You're not afraid, not after I've promised?'

She shook her head, but feebly.

'It's just that—that I feel I'm not being very sensible. How long will you want me to stay as—as your friend?' She was troubled and it showed. He took her hand in his strong brown one and gave it a little squeeze.

'Stay as long as you like,' he answered softly.

'And—and it'll stay platonic?'

'I promise.'

As long as she liked.... If he cared only a little—which he must—then the miracle was by no means impossible.

She might be his last love after all.

The sea was warm and calm; Colette had been swimming with Luke and they had both come out of the water on to the sands, their bodies scantily clad and bronzed to an Arab brown.

For the past week they had never been out of one another's company except at night. Colette, living in idyllic bliss and with hope bright in her heart, felt that the future must surely hold all that she desired, for Luke was tenderness itself, gentle, thoughtful, always at the ready to do her little services.

And it never for one moment dawned on her that all this might be an act, the careful planning of a rake whose ego had suffered a shattering blow when he had been forced to admit defeat. No, it never entered her trusting mind that Luke meant to have her, and that this stalking of his quarry was in fact proving to be a diversion of a kind never experienced before.

'Happy, sweet?' he asked with a smile as he handed her a huge beach towel, then picked one up for himself.

'So very happy, Luke,' she breathed, lifting her eyes to his, their expression revealing the tender emotion that filled her heart for him.

'So am I. You know, Jennifer, I think you and I have

met before somewhere—a long time ago.' He was rubbing himself down and missed the start she gave. It had naturally dawned upon her that, once she was sure of him, of his love and his wish to marry her, she would be forced to make a confession. But as she was confident that it would not matter, she had no qualms about it.

He came to her, when she did not answer, and took the towel from her.

'Turn around,' he commanded, and as by now she was used to obeying him she did as she was told. The towel was wrapped around; his hand at the front cupped her breasts and his lips touched her temple. She thrilled to the feel of his cool hands, the caress of his mouth, and turned in his arms to smile at him.

He began to rub her down, uncaring where his hands were but by some subtle means not giving her anything to complain about. She had often let him kiss her—had fully expected him to—but there had been little else up till now. Colette was drifting on waves of heady romance, whiling away the blissful, sunlit days, waiting for Luke to awaken to the fact that he loved her.

She had sent cards to Maisie and to Philip and his wife, saying she was having a holiday on the island, and giving them her address. She wished she was still in touch with Meriel, but her friend was now living in South America, having married and gone there soon after Colette herself was married, and somehow they had lost touch.

'There!' said Luke, throwing down the towel. 'You're all nice and dry—except for the bits of covering,' he added teasingly. She laughed but coloured too. It was strange that she felt shy, having been married, ¬nd having reached the age of twenty-five, almost.

Petros came that evening, to ask Colette over to meet his parents. He had shown surprise at her return, for he

had been told by Androula that she had gone off with
the other passengers, but he said nothing and Colette
did wonder what conclusion he had come to concern-
ing her stay at his cousin's house.

'We'll both come,' decided Luke, and Colette was
aware of Petros's sudden frown.

The house was large and luxurious but nothing like
Luke's. It was built on a small plateau, and the room
they were shown into by the smiling young maid had
a view across wooded slopes and an orange grove and
down to the sea. The gardens, like those of Luke's villa,
were a sun-drenched blaze of exotic colour from the
bougainvillaeas and Judas trees, the glorious geraniums
and chenille plants, the heliconias and allamandas.
Petros's mother was older than Colette expected, a
straight-backed lady dressed in elegant black, her hair,
thick and iron grey, taken up to form a bun at the back
of her head. She greeted Colette graciously but subjected her nephew to a strange unfathomable glance,
which he pointedly ignored by turning away. Did she
believe that Colette was his latest pillow-friend? No,
somehow Colette was convinced that she did not. Her
husband, Mr Stavros, was tall and stately, with a very
pronounced accent. He took Colette's hand, his glance
sliding to Luke, in much the same way as his wife's had
done. They all sat on the verandah and drinks were
brought to them by the maid.

'How long will you be staying?' Colette was asked by
Mr Stavros.

'Jennifer hasn't any immediate plans for leaving the
island,' interposed Luke smoothly. He stifled a yawn,
plainly uncaring whether he revealed his boredom or
not.

'Tell us about your adventure on the ship,' invited
Mrs Stavros. 'Petros did tell us quite a lot, but it's in-

teresting to hear of something like that first hand.'

Colette obliged, and afterwards there followed a period of inconsequential banalities in which Luke took scarcely any part.

'I suppose we could have asked you to dinner,' Mrs Stavros said when eventually Luke decided they must be going. 'I didn't think of it. Perhaps,' she added, looking at her nephew challengingly, 'you would like to come tomorrow evening?'

He smiled and thanked her but said he had already booked dinner at the Chelmos Hotel.

'It will be a change for Jennifer,' he ended.

When they had left and were in the car Colette asked if he really had booked a table at the hotel for dinner the following night.

'Of course. You don't think I'd lie, do you?'

She didn't know if he would or not, and the doubt troubled her. Slanting him a glance as the car was brought to a standstill on the lighted forecourt of the villa, Colette encountered an inscrutable expression. And later, at dinner, he was unusually quiet. She ventured to ask him if anything was wrong, but was immediately assured that there was nothing amiss.

It was the next morning when Colette felt she knew the reason for his change of mood. She met Petros on the beach when he was out with the dog and after a cheery greeting he seemed to fall into a state of awkwardness, of indecision. However, he spoke at last, saying anxiously,

'You remember my telling you that a girl called Stella lives over there, on that tiny island?'

She nodded, a chill in her veins.

'The girl Luke was interested in?'

'She was to have been away from Attikon for two months. She always spends two months in the summer with friends in Athens because she finds it dull here if she doesn't get a break. She came back yesterday afternoon....' His voice trailed uncertainly. 'Jennifer ... I hate the idea of your being taken in by Luke. If you were a no-good it would be different, but I don't believe you are——'

'Taken in by Luke,' she interrupted, a tremor of foreboding running through her brain. 'What do you mean, Petros?'

'Last evening I came round to Luke's place especially to try and get you on your own for a few minutes; I didn't want Luke to come over to my house, but he decided he'd come with you, so there was no chance for me to talk to you.' He stopped, then asked where Luke was now.

'On the telephone—speaking to a business associate in Athens. He said he'd be an hour at least, so I came for a walk.' She looked at him anxiously. 'You—want to—to tell me something about this Stella?' Colette had, quite naturally, thought about the girl, but, having gained considerable confidence by the way things were progressing between Luke and herself, she dismissed Stella Logara as unimportant. Luke had never cared anything for her anyway.

'Yes. You see, Jennifer, there is an understanding between them——'

'But if he fell in love with someone else——' she began involuntarily, then stopped as she noticed the expression on Petros's face. He was pitying her; his dark eyes were compassionate, and deeply anxious.

'Jennifer—Luke will never fall in love. He isn't capable. Both Mother and Father are sorry for you; they believe you're decent, that Luke hasn't—er—taken you yet—— Sorry, Jennifer, but there must be plain speaking. We don't know what made you come back and it's your own affair. But do, please, be on your guard! Mother likes you and as I said, she feels sorry for you. She said you're a sensitive child who'd be easily hurt— yes, those were her exact words,' he added as Colette looked surprised. 'Stella's come back, but Luke didn't know she was coming; he concluded she'd be away as usual for the full two months. She's not a pleasant piece,' he added grimly. 'And if she thinks you represent competition then she'll cut up rough.'

'In what way?' The question was automatic; Colette's whole mind was occupied with the other things which Petros had said. Was it true that Luke wasn't capable of falling in love? The sheer intensity of her own love, which had endured for eight long years, seemed to convince her that Luke must one day find himself loving her, madly, passionately, so that she would be bound to be his last love, the one he wished to spend the rest of his life with.

'She can be poison,' was all he would say. 'Has Luke done anything to make you think he's in love with you?'

'Yes—er—no....' Her voice faltered. 'I don't want to talk about him, Petros.' Her tone pleaded; he saw that she was almost crying, but he ignored her request as he asked,

'How long does he want you to stay?'

'I don't know——'

'I'll bet it was no longer than two months!'

'While Stella was away?' She swallowed convulsively, her heart dragging within her.

'Yes, while Stella was away.' He paused to call to the dog who was straying into the undergrowth which spread back from the belt of coconut palms that fringed the shore. 'He's not to be trusted, Jennifer,' he went on at length. 'So many women have suffered at his hands.

Mother was genuinely troubled, and said that she must find some way of warning you. Luke knew last evening that Stella was home. Father told him, when we were talking—you and Mother and I. Luke seemed a bit mad, as if her coming back had spoiled all his plans.' Another pause and then, 'I'm being callous, I suppose, but Mother stressed that I warn you. After that—well, it's entirely up to you. I'm not usually serious like this,' he added ruefully, 'but it's something I'm worried about. Luke is not to be trusted, Jennifer!' he repeated strongly.

She looked at him mistily, the weight on her heart growing heavier.

'I thought—thought he—he m-might fall in love with me.' She felt drained, and very young, as young as when she had first known Luke, and fallen in love with him. He was not for her, though. She should have known, and never been persuaded to come back.

Petros was frowning darkly.

'Don't you think you ought to leave here?' he suggested. 'He'll break your heart if you don't. I'm not being melodramatic,' he added earnestly, meeting her shadowed gaze. 'We know what he is, what he always will be—a womaniser, a rake.'

'But Stella Logara,' she found herself saying, puzzled, 'surely she objects to—to——'

'His carryings-on?' Petros shrugged his shoulders. 'Greek women expect infidelity. He's not married to her yet and so she's not in a position to complain. In any case, Luke would soon put her in her place if she even so much as tried,' he assured Colette grimly.

'You say she'll—er—cut up rough. What can she do to me?'

'I don't quite know,' he admitted after a thoughtful pause. 'But Luke's never brought one of his——' He cut himself short, then rephrased his words. 'She knows he has a reputation, but he's always kept his affairs away from this island. This business of having you in his home—well, it's amazed my parents, and me too.'

Colette said quiveringly,

'We're only friends.'

'Mother believed you were—and I must admit that this staggers us all; it's not like Luke to want any woman merely as a friend—especially a beautiful woman like you.' He paused, watching the colour slowly fuse her cheeks. 'We all believe—are firmly convinced, in fact—that he's got something up his sleeve——' He gave a shrug, a gesture which seemed to be very prevalent among Greek men, Colette had noticed. 'Why else should he have invited you to stay in his home?'

She said nothing, but in her mind the seeds of doubt and distrust had been sown. Petros and his parents ought to know Luke well, but in any case Colette had always known he had a reputation where women were concerned.

He had wanted her, desperately ... and he had gone to these lengths to get her, adopting an altogether new attitude, concealing certain characteristic traits and assuming others. He was the gentleman, kind, thoughtful, affectionate and attentive. He had kissed her, put an arm around her, given her tender glances ... and it was all an act paving the way for a final victory for him, and heartache for her. He cared nothing for this latter. In his ruthless pursuit of her as his elusive quarry his mind was set on his own triumph, and pleasure. He would take her and keep her for a couple of months—or a little less—and then, just before Stella Logara was due to arrive, he would say his careless goodbye and see her on a ship for home. Yes, that had been his original plan.

Petros was looking at her, troubled but expectant.

'Won't you take our advice and leave?' he asked when she made no attempt to speak. 'Mother said that if you do decide to leave Father will arrange everything for you.'

Colette shook her head; it was not a negative gesture but one of uncertainty. For Luke still drew her and life without him now, after this week of bliss, was too bleak and empty even to contemplate. Only now did she fully realise just how much importance she had attached to the change in Luke, to the attention he gave her.

What a naïve fool she was!

'I'll think about it, Petros,' she quivered at last, an ache of tears behind her eyes. 'I'll let you know my decision, and if I decide to leave then your father can do what's necessary for me.'

'I'll tell him—— And, Jennifer....'

'Yes?'

'Mother told me to tell you that you can stay with us if you want to leave Luke's house immediately.'

'Thank her for me,' was all Colette said, because she could not see herself moving to stay with people of whom Luke was not particularly fond. Not that she owed him any loyalty, was her instant afterthought. If in his selfishness he had no compassion for her eventual heartache, then there was no reason why she should care a scrap for any humiliation he might suffer by her leaving him and going to his aunt and uncle. Yes, she would think about it, but for the time being she decided to make no promises.

Luke was in the garden when she returned from her walk.

'I've been looking for you——' He stopped, his eyes narrowing slightly. 'Something wrong? You seem upset.'

She contrived a smile as she replied,

'Wrong, Luke? What could be wrong?'

'I don't know....' slowly and in a puzzled tone. 'You're different.'

'Tired perhaps. We were very late last night.'

He slipped an arm around her slender waist and brought her to him, aware that her body quivered, that his touch did things to her. His experience told him that, she felt sure, and squirmed within herself for her lack of ability to hide her feelings from him.

'Are you coming into the sea with me, sweet?'

Her mouth trembled. His tender voice, and the way he called her 'sweet'—they had thrilled her such a short time ago, but now....

Petros and his parents could be wrong. They were not wrong about Luke's past, of course, but it was certainly possible that they were misjudging him this time, that his motives were very different from what they suspected.

She would not jump to any hasty conclusions, condemning Luke out of hand. Her love, consuming her as it did, was too strong to be daunted without proof of his infamy.

'Yes, I'd love to,' she agreed, the anxiety clearing from her face. 'Oh, Luke—isn't it a lovely day!'

He smiled and looked skywards.

'The sun, you mean? Yes, it is a lovely day. And I'm taking you to another beach called Mandraki——'

'Mandraki,' she interrupted involuntarily. 'The harbour at Rhodes is called that.'

'There are many Mandrakis in Greece. The one on Attikon is unlike any other beach on the island; you take a delightful wooded walk to get there, and then you find this curving beach of white sand surrounded by tumbling dunes covered with grass and flowers—the lovely morning glory's rampant there. Back from the beach there's a quaint *taverna*, set romantically in a garden, and you sit at tables in this garden, with trees and vines to provide you with shade. They cook a strange but delicious concoction called a potato omelette, which is a sort of buttery mix-up, very filling and,' he added, his eyes roving her slender curves, 'very disastrous if you're a calorie-counter.'

'Which I am not,' she laughed.

His arm tightened. He cared nothing for the possibility of being seen from the house as he bent his head to kiss her.

'You've the figure of an angel,' he whispered close to her ear. 'You're the most delightful creature I've ever held in my arms.'

Colette frowned, wishing he had not reminded her of his other affairs, for it seemed that he was warning her ... warning her that she was just another of his conquests, and that nothing permanent would come of the romance.

They strolled through the shady woods hand in hand, stopping now and then so that Luke could kiss her. She sensed an impatience in him, an ardour becoming out of control. But he was still the gentleman, and if he *was* playing a part, then he was certainly a clever actor.

They reached the beach and changed in a tiny hut at the end, Colette first and then Luke. His ardent eyes roved without restraint over her lovely curves and shapely bronzed legs. He said with a trace of mocking satire,

'You do realise, my dear, that you're only just decent?'

She coloured delectably, saw his eyes burn suddenly before his lashes hid their expression from her.

'Beach fashions are like this these days,' she told him with a touch of the defensive.

'Thank heaven for the designers!' he applauded. And then, dropping the banter, 'You're too tempting, Jennifer ... and my patience is beginning to play me up.'

Was it marriage he was hinting at ... or merely the other thing?

CHAPTER NINE

THEY swam in the warm turquoise sea, had an interlude on the sands, swam again and came out finally, to sit for a while sunning themselves and getting dry.

Luke had been thoughtfully quiet, but suddenly he seemed to want to talk.

'You asked me about England,' he began reflectively, watching her closely as he added, 'I've been to many places there, most of which I can recall quite clearly—and the people I met.'

'Oh ... you can?' She was alert in every nerve, remembering that he had more than once said he thought they had met before.

'Are you no longer wanting to know about my time in England, Jennifer?'

She recalled that she had not asked about his time, but about his girl-friends, her object being to see what he had to say about her stepsister. She looked at him, sure that he was trying to recapture something elusive but important.

'No, not particularly, Luke. I expect it would not be very interesting, since you were there on business—mainly.'

His fine lips twitched at the word 'mainly', but he made no comment, asking instead where she had lived before her marriage.

She hesitated, aware that this was dangerous ground. If the time was right for her confession it would not have mattered, but the time certainly was not right, and she said quietly,

'I'd rather not talk about my life before I was married, Luke.'

He frowned in puzzlement.

'Why not? Weren't you happy?'

'I don't want to talk about it. Please respect my wishes!' Fear brought an unintentional sharpness to her voice which caused his eyebrows to shoot up arrogantly.

'There's no need to lose your temper,' he chided. 'You appear to be very touchy about the subject.'

She was sitting opposite to him, on a towel which he had spread out for her. She was hugging her knees, which were drawn up to her chin, and Luke was sitting to one side of her but some way in front, his bronzed body gleaming in the sun.

'Is it time for lunch?' she enquired. 'You did say we'd be having it here, at the *taverna*?'

The black eyes glinted at this change of subject, and his face became an angular mask. He was angry and it hurt her, receptive as she always was to his moods. Marriage to a man like him would not be all roses, she thought, hoping his anger would not last long.

And she was soon happy again, when his arm came about her as, after changing, they strolled towards the *taverna*, from where the delicious smell of Greek food drifted forth to assail their nostrils. They were given a table facing the sea, provided with a knife and fork wrapped in a paper serviette, and a glass of water.

'You have to rough it in places like this,' Luke told her with some amusement. 'They haven't got round to catering for tourists; just the locals who come out here for a bathe.'

'I like it,' she returned. 'It's the real Greece. In those places where tourism has come to be an important industry you often feel you're not in Greece at all. At

Chios we had lunch in a modern hotel and, once inside, you could have been in an hotel in London.'

'Not quite,' he corrected. 'The waiters would be very different for one thing. However,' he added, changing the subject as he took a menu from the dark stocky Greek who had come up to the table, 'let's see what they've got to offer us today.'

'The potato omelette is very good!' said the waiter.

'I'd like to try it, Luke.'

'Very well. Two potato omelettes, please.'

'Kalós! Salàta?'

'Do you want salad, Jennifer?' enquired Luke.

'Yes, please——' she stopped. 'What would I say in Greek?' she wanted to know and, when Luke told her, she glanced up into the grinning face of the waiter and said with a sort of shy hesitancy, 'Nè—er—parakaló. Is that right?'

'Né, kiria! Poli kala! Yes, you speak Greek like a native!'

He went off, still grinning, while Luke stared, taking in the soft blush, the parted lips, the translucent blue of her eyes beneath delicately-arched brows. He murmured softly,

'You send my head spinning when you look at me like that.'

Words to send her head spinning, and she expected he was well aware of it. There would be little or nothing he would not know about a woman's reactions to his flattery; or what the expression he was now wearing did to their senses ... or their hearts.

The meal was brought and when it was half-way through, four men in vraga came on to a large square board and began to dance, their hands linked by handkerchiefs, the bouzouki music being provided by a tape recorder.

'Did you enjoy it all?' Luke was walking beside her, away from the *taverna*, when he asked the question.

'It was lovely. Can we come again tomorrow?'

'Perhaps,' he said non-committally.

They reached the shore; the light was brilliant, the sea slightly choppy, foaming like green soda-water. Luke took her along a green valley and they stopped by a watermill. He told her what it was like here in spring.

'There are wide expanses of blue iris growing up the hillsides, and yellow gorse and mustard and sorrel. Anemones of every colour, and primulas—all growing wild. And those trees you see there are almonds; they cover the whole of that side of the valley with pink.' He looked down at her, the shadow from the mill making his face look more austere than ever, more pagan-like. She thought of his name ... which in ancient legend meant 'demon god'.

Lucifer ... who had picked a rose, then tossed it away, who had said, when on an impulse she never had been able to understand she had retrieved it and offered it to him,

'Keep it. What on earth would I want with it?'

And she had kept it, pretending that he had picked it especially for her.

'Shall I see it in the spring, I wonder?' The words came softly, involuntarily, born of a yearning that was almost physically painful.

He took her in his arms, and pressed his lips to hers.

'Spring,' he murmured, his lips caressing her ear, 'is a long time off. This is now, my love ... and we are wasting precious time.'

She stiffened in his arms.

'What—what is it you want?' She knew it was not marriage. The knowledge seemed to crucify her, searing her heart and mind with pain. Petros and his parents were right: Luke had been playing with her. And she now knew that the doubts instilled by Petros had been circling the edge of her mind all the time she had been swimming with Luke, all through lunch, even though she had tried desperately to thrust them away.

'You know what I want, Jennifer; you're neither a fool nor an innocent schoolgirl. How long do you suppose you can resist me?' he asked with a sort of mocking satire. His eyes were mocking, too, as they stared into hers. 'Accept your fate, and come to me.' His lips found hers again, capturing them swiftly as if he expected some resistance. 'You're intoxicating. I want you, sweet, and there's no use your denying that you want me——' He held her from him, insistence in his sudden silence. She turned her head away, but it was brought round again with a masterful gesture that thrilled even while it annoyed. 'You are not honest with yourself, Jennifer. If you were, you'd stop this nonsense and enjoy what's there for the taking.'

She said quietly,

'You made a solemn promise that, if I agreed to be your guest, it would remain platonic.'

An exasperated sound almost like a hiss escaped him.

'You must have known we couldn't go on like that indefinitely.'

'I certainly didn't know that, within just over a week, you'd want to go back on your word!' She was angry now, wishing—for the very first time—that she did not love him, because then she could have quarrelled, told him just what kind of a man he was. But if they must part then she could not take with her memories that would bring even more pain than what she was now suffering. She would say goodbye in her own way, leaving no animosity behind her, so that when he remembered her—which she knew he would now and then—he'd see her as she really was, not a woman torn by anger.

'Are you so naïve?' he queried impatiently. 'Did you genuinely believe that we'd never make love?'

No, she hadn't believed any such thing. She had cherished the hope, that with time on her side, she would have made him love her, and offer her marriage. But she did not have time on her side; Luke had cut it short. In any case, her dreams were as dust from the start, since he had merely wanted her back so that he could bring her to his feet.

'I think,' she said, drawing right away from him, 'we'd better go back to the villa. I'm going home, back to England. Meanwhile,' she added, actually wanting to do and say something that would hurt and annoy, 'I shall stay with your aunt and uncle. They'll have me——'

'My aunt and uncle?' he cut in raspingly. 'What do you mean, they'll have you?'

She was pale but composed, a quiet dignity about her which he had never seen before.

'If you must know, they've already offered me their hospitality. I shall accept it and stay with them until your uncle gets me a ship or a flight.'

Luke's teeth gritted together. She saw the crimson streaks that fused into the burnished bronze of his cheeks.

'You will not stay with them!' he thundered. 'How—and when—did you come to make these arrangements with them?'

'Petros saw me this morning. His mother had asked him to see me, to warn me about you——'

'Warn? What the hell has he been saying about me?'

'Only the truth, Luke,' she answered, her eyes misty with tears. 'They knew you were playing a game with me, and because they suspected too that I was not your type of woman, they were troubled about me. I'm grateful to them——'

'They're interfering old busybodies who've always poked their noses into my affairs——' He stopped, then said, as the thought occurred to him, 'You've known all morning that you were intending to leave me? That was why you were looking upset, why you wouldn't answer when I asked you what was wrong! Well, let me impress this on you: you are *not* going to stay with my aunt and uncle!'

Her eyes blazed. She had tolerated all she was going to tolerate from him. To the devil with her intention of fading peacefully out of his life!

'You can't dictate to me!' she flashed. 'Who do you think you are to adopt an attitude like this? Anyone would think I was one of your poor spineless Greek women who cringe at every harsh word their lords and masters speak! You've just said I'm neither a fool nor an innocent schoolgirl—well, you were right! Trusting I might have been, but I'm now admitting that you're rotten through and through! Women are just toys to be played with until you tire of them, and then you toss them aside, crushing them in the process! You've lost this time, though! I've been cleverer than you; I've escaped!'

Silence, palpable and tense. Colette ventured a glance at his dark face. It was taut and harsh; his eyes like black onyx, his thin nostrils flaring. He was all Greek at this moment, a true product of the pagans of old. But, strangely, he did not frighten her. She seemed to have acquired an armour of reserve and dignity which neither his fury nor his persuasion—should he resort to it again—could pierce. Just as she had known where she was going before, she knew again now. But

this time there would be no turning back. It was goodbye, for ever. She had a beautiful home and loyal
servants; she would find peace from the turmoil which
this past fortnight had brought to her. Yes, there were
compensations. And she was young; she would get over
it.

'You've escaped, you say?' Luke's rasping voice, coming through the silence, caught at her nerves, scraping
them. 'The game's not finished yet!' he told her implacably. 'One thing is for sure! You're not going to
stay with my aunt and uncle!'

'You've already said that,' she reminded him. 'And I
have said that I shall please myself! You're nothing to
me—get that! Nothing!'

'You ... liar, Jennifer.' There was a staggering
change in his tone, and in his features, a thin smile
easing the compression of his mouth, a sort of mocking
censure replacing the hardness of his eyes. She caught
her breath, furious with herself for the emotions that
were again stirring within her. The power of the man
was too dangerous! She was drawn to him even now,
when she believed her mind was fully made up. 'Can
you look me in the eye and say I mean nothing to you?'

She was close to tears, but by some miracle she
managed to adopt an air of levity as she flashed back at
him,

'How pompous you are, Luke! Are you trying to say
I'm in love with you?'

'Not in love, no. But you're as attracted to me as I
am to you. The trouble is that you refuse to admit it—
and so we're at stalemate.'

So he was not so perceptive after all. Colette would
not have been surprised if he had discovered that she
was in love with him.

'Then stalemate it remains,' she assured him, still in that light tone of voice.

'You're a wretch, Jennifer,' he said softly after a long pause during which his patience seemed to be strained almost beyond endurance. 'You asked just now what I wanted of you. I think I must ask what you want of me?' She made no answer and he went on, 'My instinct tells me that you had something else in mind when you agreed to come back to me.'

'Something else?' she repeated, stressing the second word.

'Something besides the holiday you were having ... besides the platonic part of it.'

'Why should your instinct tell you that?' she asked interestedly.

'Because it didn't make sense,' was his swift and disparaging rejoinder. 'You really wanted to come back here, but why? You must have had a reason.'

'The holiday,' she murmured, only now realising that her action must not have been very logical in his eyes. But then he was ignorant of her motives, of her fruitless hopes.

'You were contemplating an affair but felt you hadn't known me long enough,' he stated emphatically.

'Have it your own way, Luke. If I hadn't know you long enough then I still haven't known you long enough. It's only just over a week since I came back, remember.'

'You're telling me my deductions are all wrong?'

'I'm not telling you anything.' She was tired of the argument, and she turned away, saying she was going back to the villa to pack. 'I want to leave today—at once.'

'I can't have you leaving me in this way,' he snapped.

'What are people going to conclude? This is a very tiny island and gossip can be injurious.'

'Do you care for gossip, Luke? You amaze me!'

'Be yourself,' he rasped. 'I dislike you when you try to be smart!'

She coloured at the rebuke and fell silent.

'I've said I shan't allow you to go. I'll see my aunt and explain. She's a fool anyway, to have thought for one moment I'd leave myself open to gossip of that kind.'

Something quite beyond her control made Colette retort,

'Is it Stella you're afraid of? She would be affected by the gossip?'

His eyes glinted dangerously.

'Has Petros been telling you about Stella—about her coming home earlier than she should have done?'

'He did say something about it, yes.'

'I'll see him, and at once!' he said between his teeth.

Colette walked away, but he soon caught her up. That he was concerned by her decision to leave the villa was plain to see. She herself had not thought of the gossip that might result from such a move as she contemplated, and as she had no wish to embarrass Luke she promised to give the matter a little more thought before making a firm decision.

She had not expected to be going out to dine at the hotel that evening, and she was in denims and a short-sleeved blouse when, at eight o'clock, Luke tapped lightly on her bedroom door.

'Can I come in, Jennifer?'

'Yes.' She moved from the window where she had been standing, staring out at the deep purple dome of the sky, where a million stars shone, the moon in their midst.

'Why aren't you ready?' he asked, his eyes flitting over her. 'Have you forgotten we're going to the hotel for dinner? I've booked for us to eat at half-past eight.'

'You don't expect me to come with you?' she said in surprise, angry with herself for wanting to go with him, for being glad that he had come for her. He was superbly dressed in oyster-white linen and a pampas-green shirt, his hair gleaming as usual. She felt shabby beside him, unkempt, and inferior.

'Certainly I expect you to come with me,' he answered with some asperity. 'Don't be so childish, Jennifer. The sulks don't become you!'

Her chin lifted at his words, but before she had time to think of anything fitting to say he was speaking again, telling her to hurry up and get ready. At this imperious order she did find something to say.

'Don't give me orders! I've a good mind not to come with you!'

At which he strode purposefully across the room.

'If you aren't downstairs in fifteen minutes,' he warned in a very soft voice, 'I shall come up and give you a little assistance in getting ready!'

The hotel lounge was small and cosy, and most of the people were natives of the island. But some strangers were present and it was soon discovered that a ship had come in that day bringing about twenty holidaymakers who were 'island-hopping' in the Aegean.

'Some of them are staying here and the others at the Pantheon on the other side of the island,' a young man told Luke with a grim smile. 'I hope we're not going to be "discovered", because Attikon will soon be spoiled. It isn't big enough for crowds of tourists.' He had come up to Luke the moment he entered the lounge and was introduced to Colette, Luke saying that she was a friend of his who was having a holiday with him. The man, Mitso Palisides, assumed a wooden expression and accepted Luke's invitation to join them for drinks.

'I don't think there's any fear of that,' Luke assured him. 'We have had these island-hoppers before, but they've been gone in a couple of days.'

'These are here for a week. They're on some kind of a package tour, from England. The tour started at Piraeus and lasts three weeks altogether.'

Luke shrugged; he wasn't interested, and the conversation turned on to other topics. The menus were brought and passed to Colette and Luke. Mitso was not here for dinner, he said.

He went off within a few minutes and they were left alone. Luke caught Colette looking at him and smiled. She could not respond, for her heart was too heavy. He frowned, then, and gave all his attention to the menu.

'Luke!' The voice was husky and low, its owner a slender girl with swaying hips and jet black hair. She wore diamonds and pearls at her throat and on her wrists; her matching earrings were about four inches long. 'I wondered if I should find you here!'

'Stella.' He rose at once, his face a mask. It was impossible for Colette even to hazard a guess at his feelings. 'I knew you were back, of course. Meet a friend of mine, Jennifer Maddox, from England.'

The girl's expression was hidden beneath heavily-mascaraed lashes, the hand she extended was long and slender and brown, with perfectly-manicured nails.

'How do you do, Miss Maddox.'

'It's Mrs Maddox,' corrected Luke. 'My omission. Jennifer's a widow.' He was smoothly composed, totally unruffled by what must be an unexpected meeting.

'A widow?' repeated the husky voice as Stella sat down. 'You're young to be a widow, Mrs Maddox.'

'Yes....' Colette felt small and inadequate, overwhelmed by this girl who oozed self-confidence and poise.

'Are you here for dinner?' asked Luke after clapping his hands for a waiter.

'Yes; Father will be here shortly.' She spoke with an accent which was very pronounced, and when the waiter arrived she gave Luke no time to ask what she wanted but gave the order herself, in Greek. And then she said something in Greek to Luke, who slid his eyes in Colette's direction. She coloured, wondering what had been said. Something disparaging? Impossible to read anything from Luke's inscrutable countenance.

Stella's father arrived and it was decided that the four of them would dine together, a circumstance which spoiled the meal entirely for Colette. But this was nothing in comparison to what was to come. When, after the meal was over, they returned to the lounge for a final drink, it was to find that those tourists who were staying at the Pantheon had come over from the other side of the island to join their friends.

And almost the first person Colette's eyes alighted on was Elspeth. She gave a little gasp of disbelief, her heart lurching as if it had escaped its moorings.

She glanced swiftly at Luke, but he had not noticed her. However Elspeth, glancing around as she stood at the bar, a glass of whisky in her hand, suddenly saw him and without even a word to those she was with, sailed over to the table at which he and his companions were sitting.

'Luke—hello!' she crooned in that voice which Colette had once come to hate. 'When they said we were stopping here I wondered if we would meet again!

How are you——?' She stopped, to glance at his three companions in turn. Colette held her breath. It was crazy, she knew, and yet she was waiting for her step-sister to recognise her. But of course there was no recognition whatsoever in her eyes. 'I'm sorry for the intrusion,' she purred, 'but I'm sure I'll be forgiven. Luke and I are old friends,' she ended, embracing them all in one sweeping glance. Colette, after the first violent shock, felt she wanted to burst out laughing. For here was Luke, rake and womaniser, in the company of no fewer than three of them!

Her lips twitched. This was going to be amusing, she thought, waiting for Luke to speak, while at the same time aware of the grim evidence of jealousy in Stella's eyes. All through dinner she herself had come in for malicious glances, though the Greek girl was, on the whole, perfectly in command of her feelings. But for her to be faced with another one——!

Luke, sliding Colette a glance, could not but notice that she was suppressing laughter, and she saw his eyes narrow as if he were sending her a grim warning. But the next moment he himself was obviously appreciating this situation and his own lips twitched. However, his voice and manner were perfectly cool and politely detached as he began to make the introductions. Colette saw Elspeth's eyes roving over her, taking in the model evening gown she was wearing, another Paris creation, this time of coral-coloured lace over a white under-skirt. The jewellery she had chosen was the diamond and sapphire necklace and bracelet and earrings given her by Uncle Patrick on her twenty-first birthday. Elspeth's final glance took in the wedding-ring Colette was wearing and an expression of puzzlement crossed her face momentarily.

Stella was plainly furious when Elspeth said purr-ingly,

'Didn't we have fun, Luke, in those days when we went about together? It was in England,' she explained for everyone's benefit.

'How long ago?' enquired Stella, forcing a thin smile. Colette watched Mr Logara; he was totally lacking in interest and she was not at all surprised when, spotting an acquaintance at the bar, he muttered a quiet 'excuse me' and took himself off.

'Oh, ages,' answered Elspeth airily, taking the seat offered by Luke who in turn took over the one vacated by Stella's father. 'About eight years—isn't it, Luke?' She took a drink and placed her glass on the table, leaving her hands free to take cigarettes from her bag and light one. Colette saw her left hand for the first time. She wore a ring on her third finger, but it was neither a wedding ring nor an engagement ring. Just a dress ring, which Colette remembered. It had belonged to Elspeth's mother.

'I believe it was about eight years ago,' agreed Luke, lifting a hand to conceal a yawn. So he was bored, was he? Colette's eyes were alight with amusement. She was enjoying all this in spite of the heavy weight dragging at her heart.

'Eight years,' murmured Stella. 'I didn't know you at that time, did I, Luke?'

'No, Stella, we hadn't met. Your father built his house here about five years ago, if my memory is not at fault.'

'That's right, it is five years since we came to live on Attikon.' She turned to Elspeth. 'You and Luke haven't seen one another, then, for eight years?'

Elspeth shook her head.

'No, yet it doesn't seem that long, does it, Luke?'

He glanced at her; Colette, remembering clearly the last time they were together, wondered if he were remembering too.

'I'm afraid I never bother my head much about time, Elspeth,' he drawled in a bored voice. 'It passes, and there's nothing to be gained in trying to assess its speed.'

Elspeth rode the snub without the trace of a blush, turning her attention to Colette.

'You're English. Are you on holiday?' Again her eyes flickered over her, envy lurking in their depths. She was thirty-three now, Colette remembered, and she had lost some of the beauty she had once flaunted before the girl who, she had prophesied with a sneer, would be very lucky if she were to find a husband. And if she did, Elspeth had said, he would be nothing better than one of the agricultural labourers who worked on the farms nearby. It was just like Elspeth to look down on farm workers, thought Colette who, herself, had some fine men working on her own farm in Devon.

'Yes,' she answered coolly, 'I'm on holiday.'

Elspeth had picked up her glass but as Colette spoke her hand stopped with it half way to her lips. Something had caught her attention. Colette sensed it immediately, even without the flickering stare she was receiving from her puzzled eyes.

'You're in the hotel—this hotel?'

'No, I'm staying with Luke, as his guest.' She could not help it, but there was a sort of malicious satisfaction in Colette's next words. 'It's a beautiful white and blue villa in the most incredibly beautiful grounds. I'm very lucky to be staying there.'

The glass was taken to Elspeth's mouth, very slowly. There was a tenseness in the air which no one could possibly miss. It was dispelled by the reappearance of Stella's father, who said he wanted to go home. Stella frowned but got up.

'I'll say goodnight to you all.' Her glance swept

around the three left at the table. 'Shall I be seeing you tomorrow, Luke?'

'I don't know, Stella. I'm thinking of going to Athens, but I don't know quite when.'

'Oh....' Stella shrugged, repeated her goodnights, then turned to follow her father who, having said his own rather sour goodnights, was striding away towards the door.

'I'd love to see your house, Luke,' Elspeth said silkily. 'I'm here for a week, staying at the Pantheon, so I have plenty of time. Won't you invite me, just for old times' sake?' She was speaking to Luke but her eyes were fixed on Colette's hair. Tension was in the air again. Luke, his eyes drawn to Colette's hair by Elspeth's prolonged stare, was frowning, unable to understand what it was that affected the atmosphere. As for Colette—she was enjoying herself because she had her stepsister totally puzzled. It was obviously the voice that had first caused that little access of interest and perplexity. Elspeth, un-like Luke, had known her voice well, whereas Luke, apart from that one evening after the wedding, had scarcely heard Colette speak at all, simply because he showed so little interest that no opportunity arose for her to carry on a conversation with him. Colette be-lieved that her voice had changed anyway; it must have done in eight years. But there must also be a similarity to the way she had spoken before, and it was this similarity which Elspeth had noticed.

Luke was frowning; he might not have heard his old flame's request, so little notice did he take of it.

It was Colette, fired with a sense of mischief totally at variance with her true character, who said persuas-ively,

'Do invite Miss Whitney, Luke. It would be nice for you both to have a chat, just for old times' sake.'

He threw her a suspicious glance, his face impassive. She knew instinctively that he was baffled but yet had no idea why he should be.

'How kind of you,' purred Elspeth. 'It will be a nice diversion for me, because I'm travelling alone.'

'Do you often travel?' asked Colette conversationally.

'I have done lately, since my father died; that was two and a half years ago.'

'You live alone?' Colette amazed herself by her confidence. Elspeth being questioned! It would have been unheard-of in the old days. Colette would instantly have been put in her place.

'I do, yes.'

Colette wondered why she had never married; she had certainly been beautiful enough to have had her pick.

'You had no brothers and sisters?'

Luke shot her a glance, his eyes alert, piercing. She smiled sweetly at him, then looked at Elspeth, waiting for her answer.

'No—er—not of my own. My father married a widow with a young daughter——'

'Oh, that would be nice for you!' Colette managed to get in quickly.

Elspeth frowned, her lips compressing.

'It wasn't, as a matter of fact. We had nothing in common.'

'What a shame. It could have been rather wonderful —for all four of you.'

Elspeth and Luke exchanged glances. Elspeth was becoming uncomfortable and Colette, still fired with mischief, and a burning desire to disconcert the girl who, with her father, had caused her and her mother so much misery, looked hard at her, forcing her to make some comment.

'It could—yes. But the woman was a slut and the daughter so ugly that I'm afraid she gave me the creeps.'

Colette turned her lovely eyes to Luke's face. She knew he would hate the word slut and was amazed that Elspeth had used it. He would not care for the last part of the sentence, either. But as before his face was inscrutable. He seemed detached, distant, yet she knew without a doubt that his brain was alert, that he was not missing one word of what was being spoken. She said to Elspeth, lifting her brows in a gesture of surprise,

'Your father married a woman like that? How very strange. Didn't he know she was a—a—well, that sort of a woman before he married her?'

'Oh, she was pretty then, and smart. She let herself go.'

'How sad for you. It must have been a great trial. And this daughter? What was——?'

'I'd rather not talk about it,' interrupted Elspeth, flushing under Luke's unsmiling stare. 'It's all in the past. They left us in the lurch and we never spoke of them afterwards.'

At this Luke's expression became one of interest.

'They left you?'

'You knew them?' interposed Colette, feigning surprise.

He nodded.

'Yes, I knew them—just a little.'

Colette decided she had gone far enough, for the present. She did not care for Luke's expression; he was well enough acquainted with her ways to know she was acting out of character in putting pertinent questions to a total stranger. So she changed the subject, reverting to what had been said before.

'Are you going to invite Miss Whitney to your villa, Luke?'

There was only the slightest hesitation before he said, in that finely-timbred, accented voice which Colette had always found so very attractive,

'Yes, certainly. Shall we make it tomorrow?'

'That would be lovely,' from Elspeth who, having finished her cigarette, was lighting another. 'In the afternoon?'

'If you like,' he began, when Colette interrupted him.

'Why not for dinner?' she smiled. For dinner she could look her very best, as she had some beautiful evening gowns. She could also wear some other jewellery, in addition, dinner at the villa was always something special, with candles and flowers and quiet *bouzouki* music. Elspeth would know what she had missed by losing Luke.

'I'm a cat,' she said to herself wonderingly. 'A bitchy, horrid cat—and I like it!'

CHAPTER TEN

LUKE was exceptionally quiet during the drive from the hotel back to the villa, and Colette was left to her own thoughts. That afternoon she had enquired about boats going to Piraeus, and had been told that if she wanted to go direct she would have to wait four days for the *Apollo*. She could go on one of the smaller boats, but as they called at other islands on the way, the voyage would not only take longer but would be tedious as well. So she reluctantly decided to wait for the *Apollo*. It was a difficult decision because, although the parting from Luke would tear her to pieces, she was most sensible of the fact that every minute in his presence was temptation, for she was sure he would never give up until the very last moment.

However, she was glad now she had not been able to get a boat, because this evening had been most diverting, and there was the promise of more to come. For the first time she had experienced the satisfaction, not only of holding her own with Elspeth, but of actually disconcerting her. And tomorrow evening there would be a repetition, since Colette had every intention of continuing to play the game she had started. And if in the process Elspeth and Luke should discover who she was, then what did it matter? She, Colette, was leaving here and would never see Luke again, so if he learned she was that ugly little girl he had once scorned and derided, laughing when Elspeth said she had a 'crush' on him, it was of no consequence at all. As for Elspeth—well, Colette rather thought she would enjoy her stepsister's reaction to the knowledge that the girl she had subjected to such contempt was now beautiful. Yes, tomorrow evening promised to bring the sweet reward of revenge, and Colette, kind and gentle as she had always been, was at the same time human.

Of course, it was possible—most probable, in fact— that neither Elspeth nor Luke would make a guess at her identity. There was no real reason why they should, and Colette rather relished the idea of their being puzzled—as they were already, she thought in some amusement, as she cast Luke a sideways glance—and yet not being able to fathom what they were puzzled about.

Yes, decided Colette, whether they guessed or not, tomorrow evening would be most enjoyable!

The villa came into view through a cluster of coconut palms, a lovely white and blue home with arches and patios, with shady courtyards and exotic gardens, tended by an army of gardeners. There were terraces and parterres, a sunken rose garden, a swimming-pool shaded by jacaranda trees and flaring crimson hibiscus bushes. Luke had his own private beach, with a jetty on the end where his luxury motor launch was moored.

He turned into an avenue of tarmarind trees and brought the car to a smooth halt outside the porticoed front door. The white marble steps shone in the headlights' glare before he switched them off, to leave the forecourt less brightly lit, for Davos had left only one light on.

'Well——' He turned in his seat and looked at her. 'Did you enjoy it?'

'Very much. Thank you for taking me, Luke,' Colette answered demurely.

His eyes were filled with suspicion.

'Something requires explaining,' he said brusquely.

'Oh?' with well-feigned bewilderment. 'What needs explaining, Luke?'

'Have you ever seen that girl before?'

'Stella?' She shook her head. 'No——'

'Elspeth!' he snapped.

She swallowed, annoyed by her own hesitation, which he was bound to notice. She thought of the possibility of the truth coming out and hated to lie. On the other hand, if she said yes to his question all the rest would have to come out now, at this moment, and her fun would be spoilt.

'Why should you think we'd met before?' she prevaricated, having decided to keep up the pretence as long as she could. 'It seems a strange thing to say, Luke.'

'There have been several strange things said this evening,' he growled. She looked at him and wanted to laugh. He was so furious at his own bewilderment. He was always so clever!—always perceptive, quick to grasp things. But now he was finding that he was not so clever after all!

'I don't understand?' she said.

'I could shake you,' he rejoined softly, and opened the car door.

'Have I done something to offend you?' she enquired innocently when he came round to open her door for her. They stood close, Luke staring down into her face, his eyes narrowed, his mouth compressed. He looked at her hair. It was short now, whereas it had been long eight years ago, down to her shoulders. It was the same colour, though ... and her hair was a particularly attractive colour, honey-gold. It also waved slightly, so that the ends flicked up. They did that when it was long; they still did it even though it was short.

'You've done many things to offend me,' said Luke

at last—'and I'm not talking about tonight.' He took
her hand, drawing her away from the car. 'You really
intend leaving me in four days' time?' His lips were on
her hair; she thrilled to the nearness of him, lifting her
face, yearning for his kiss. It was madness! He would
tempt her and she would have to fight him again. But
he did not tempt her. He merely kissed her gently on
the lips, then, patting her cheek rather harder than
necessary, he said shortly, 'You're a mystery to me,
Jennifer! I've just asked you a question!' he added imperiously. 'Answer it.'

'Of course I'm leaving. I can't stay here for ever.'

'You could stay longer.'

'What about Stella? Petros told me that you expected
her to be away for two months. That's why you asked
me to stay for two months.'

'I didn't ask you to stay for two months! No specific
time was mentioned!' He was furious because she had
mentioned Stella, telling him what Petros had said.

'I thought it was to be two months,' she said.

'Why?'

'Well ... I——'

'You didn't know about Stella at that time, so you
couldn't have thought it was to be for two months!'

She said, puzzled,

'What is this all about, Luke? I don't understand
you at all.'

'Then that makes two of us,' he snapped, dropping
her hand. 'There's been something about you which I
could not understand, right from the first. You're deep,
I'm thinking—damned deep!'

She coloured but ignored his words as she said,

'Was it to be more than two months, Luke?'

'Of course it was!'

'But why——?'

'Do you suppose I could tire of you in two months?' he interrupted furiously.

Colette was trembling all over.

'What about—about Stella?' She had not meant to say anything like that at all, but the question came from the back of her mind and was out before she realised it.

'Stella means nothing to me!'

Colette stared at him.

'But you told me there was a possibility of your marrying her,' she reminded him.

'I didn't say it was her——'

'No, I remember that,' she broke in impatiently. 'But it was Stella we were talking about at the time.'

He admitted it, then fell silent.

Her trembling increased.

'And now?' she murmured, looking up into his dark forbidding face.

'I've decided not to marry her!'

'But—why——?'

'It's time for bed,' he cut in roughly. 'Come on in! Do you expect me to stand out here all night!'

Colette gaped at him.

'Well,' she flashed, 'I like that! It wasn't I who wanted to stay out! It's been a long day, and so many things have happened, and for your information—I'm tired! So why have *you* kept *me* out here all this time!'

'If you're so damned tired then go to bed!' He strode away, leaving her with tears in her eyes and bewilderment in her heart.

The purple shades of twilight were clothing the sleepy landscape when the taxi swept along the drive. Colette, superb in a long dress of finely-embroidered cotton, and with a diamond necklace at her throat and a star in her hair, stood on the patio and watched the car draw right up to the front door and stop. Elspeth got out, paid the driver, then stood for a long moment, looking at the beautiful façade of the villa. Colette, in the shadows, waited for her to move, which she did, but it was only to swing around, making a full circle as she took in the immediate grounds, floodlit, with the fountain sparkling and the statuary of white marble gleaming but faintly indistinct, giving it a ghostly appearance which seemed to add to the magic and mystery of the atmosphere. From the sea a fresh breeze drifted in, gathering the flower perfumes as it passed over the villa grounds. The moon was coming up from behind the hills, filtering the wispy cirrus clouds and making a tapestry of light and shade on the lawn. And over all was the deep silence which so appealed to Colette, a silence rarely broken by anything other than the shrilling of cicadas in the olive trees, the sough of the wind through a cluster of palms, or the sad and lonely cry of a donkey on the drowsy hillside.

She watched her stepsister turn again, stand another moment, then mount the wide steps to the front door. One of the maids opened it seconds after the bell was rung; Colette moved into the room, walking across it to the hall.

'Good evening, Elspeth,' she heard Luke say, and for some reason she stopped before reaching the door into the hall, which was slightly ajar.

'Hello, Luke! Oh, but you have a beautiful house here!'

'I like it,' brusquely before he asked if he could take her wrap. 'You didn't need it,' he was saying. 'Nights at this time of the year are always warm and balmy.'

'I've never been to Greece before, so I wouldn't know.'

A small silence ensued and then, in a much quieter and guarded tone,

'That young lady—your friend, Luke. Who is she?'

'Why do you ask?' Luke's tone was sharp, inquisitive.

'I'm puzzled about her. There's something faintly familiar——' She stopped and Colette could almost see the shake of her head, a gesture of bafflement. 'Jennifer.... The name isn't familiar. Have you known her long, Luke?'

'Not too long,' he replied non-committally.

'Where does she come from?'

'Devon.' There was a question in the one brief word; Luke was half hoping to get some information, but all Elspeth said was that she did not know anyone in Devon.

'She has no parents,' added Luke, endeavouring to prompt her memory. 'She's been widowed for about three and a half years. Her husband was a very wealthy man. He left her a mansion and a vast estate.'

'No.... I had a feeling I'd met her somewhere, but I'd remember someone like that.' A pause and then, 'Her voice and hair remind me of——' She stopped, swinging round as Colette, spurred to action, came through the door, a smile of welcome on her lovely face.

'You're nice and early, Miss Whitney. I'm glad! Can we have drinks outside, Luke?' She smiled into his eyes, saw the glimmer of frustration in them and could have laughed. An imp had got into her, taking her over, precipitating her to mischief, imbuing her with a roguish desire to have fun at someone else's expense.

'If you wish, Jennifer,' he said.

'It's such a beautiful evening.'

'It is.'

'Shall I take Miss Whitney's wrap for you?'

He looked down at her from his great height, an enigmatical expression on his face. Colette had kept right out of his way all day, leaving the villa very early, asking Androula to give him the message that she was going for a ramble over the island and would be having her lunch out. She would be back in time for dinner but not before. And she had done just that, arriving back with just enough time to spare for a bath and to get ready for dinner. So this was the first time she and Luke had met since he walked away from her last night in the garden.

'No,' he said shortly, and clapped his hands. 'Davos will take it.'

However, it was Androula who came in answer to the imperious summons and the wrap was handed over.

'We'll have drinks on the terrace,' he told the maid, then turned to the two girls. 'We'll go out. The chairs and table will be taken out directly.' He was suave now, fully in command of himself, as if, though filled with vexation, he was not intending to allow it to dominate his mind to the exclusion of all else. Elspeth was looking at him, fascinated by him, and Colette could sense all the old feeling, the desire to win him for herself. The girl's eyes slid to Colette momentarily; she was wondering about her position here, probably concluding that she was Luke's latest mistress. Strangely, the idea held no embarrassment for Colette. On the contrary, she felt elated at the notion of making Elspeth jealous of her, for she knew without the smallest doubt that her stepsister would gladly change places with her if she could.

They strolled out on to the terrace, the cool breeze on their faces, tousling Luke's hair a little and taking some of the severity away, giving him a more human look. He wore a suit of grey mohair, with the collar and cuffs of his white shirt contrasting vividly with the copper-bronze of his skin. Elspeth kept on glancing at him from under her beautiful curling lashes.

The drinks were brought out by Davos and placed on the table, which had a few moments ago been brought from the house.

'Have you had a good day, Miss Whitney?' It was Colette who spoke first, after they were all seated at the table.

'Yes, it was most pleasant. We all swam and lazed about on the beach. There isn't much else to do from what I can gather. It's very restful, though,' she added hastily, as if she suddenly feared she had offended Luke.

'I find it restful too,' agreed Colette. 'But of course I'm here, in this tranquil setting. Don't you adore Luke's villa?' She flashed him an open, charming smile, but his eyes merely narrowed and glinted. 'It's not possible to appreciate the grounds with just the floodlights on, but I assure you they're fantastically beautiful!' Again she flashed Luke a smile. She heard the intake of his breath, saw him lean back in his chair, hitch up a trouser leg automatically, and fix her with a penetrating stare.

'I'm sure they must be,' from Elspeth in a voice that had a rasping quality about it now. 'Have you been here long, Mrs Maddox?'

'Just about ten days.'

'Oh ... I had the impression that you'd been here some time.' Elspeth flicked open a gold case and extracted a long cigarette which she inserted into a holder. 'Shall you be staying indefinitely?'

Probing, was she? And not very subtle about it either.

Colette sent Luke a questioning glance.

'How long shall I be staying?' she queried, throwing the ball into his court.

She thought she heard a tiny hiss but could not be

sure. His voice in any case was smooth and cool as he replied,

'You are fully aware, my dear, that you can stay as long as you like.'

She had expected an answer like that, because, of course, it was true.

'I'm so very lucky—don't you think so, Miss Whitney?'

'Yes,' curtly as Elspeth drew deeply on her cigarette. 'You are.'

Luke said, a sort of malicious challenge in his tone,

'How long *are* you staying, Jennifer?'

She looked down, avoiding his penetrating black eyes.

'Oh,' airily, 'I haven't decided yet.'

'You have commitments at home?' from Elspeth, who was suddenly intent, her head cocked as if she wanted to make sure she could hear Colette's voice clearly.

'Of course. Everyone has commitments.'

'I've mentioned to Elspeth that you own a large mansion and estate,' interjected Luke, reaching for his glass.

'You manage it all yourself?'

'No, Miss Whitney. I have an excellent manager on the farm, and under him, some equally excellent employees.' Colette felt so poised, so self-confident. And it was with a hint of pride not unmingled with arrogance that she added, 'The house is well taken care of by my housekeeper and a couple of maids.' Another glance in Luke's direction and she was taking in his frown. He could not make her out at all, since this was tantamount to boasting, and he knew that such conduct was totally alien to her character. Last night he had strongly suspected that she had met Elspeth before; he was now convinced of it. Colette had no doubts about that at all. But what was puzzling him was why Elspeth found it impossible to place *her*. There were many other questions he would like answered, she knew, and it was gratifying to think she could keep him guessing!

'Your husband left you all that, Luke was telling me. He must have been very wealthy?' Colette elected to let that pass, and sat sipping her drink and waiting for Elspeth to add something to it. 'He must have died young, Mrs Maddox ... or perhaps he was a great many years older than you?'

So ... the claws were coming out, were they? With fine unconcern Colette put down her glass, fixed her stepsister with a haughty stare and murmured slowly,

'My husband was under thirty when he died, Miss Whitney. Some women would marry an old man for his money, but as I don't happen to rate it as of very much importance at all, the last thing I would do is marry for money, whether the man was old or not.'

Elspeth coloured, put her cigarette between her lips and inhaled deeply. Colette continued to fix her eyes, wondering if she were remembering her assertion that she intended to marry a millionaire—and that if he had a title so much the better.

'I think,' said Luke with a darkling glance at Colette, 'that it's time we were going indoors. Dinner will be served in five minutes or so.'

The moon was high as they walked back to the lighted forecourt, its magical glow showering the grounds and the beach and the sea with a silver luminescence. The breeze stirring the palm fronds was like music, the flower perfumes heady. Colette, walking beside Luke, yearned to be alone with him, in a romantic setting such as this, yearned for the strength of his arms, the pleasure-pain of his lips, the words that would send her head spinning.

A sigh escaped her and he seemed to know, for he turned swiftly, a question in his eyes.

Elspeth was on his other side, staring straight ahead, taking no notice of either of them, and Colette rather thought that already she was regretting having sought the invitation.

They had just entered the house when Davos appeared to announce that dinner was ready. In the dining-room there were candles only, for illumination —over twenty of them, ten of which occupied two five-branch silver candelabra, one at each end of the table. Silver place mats and coasters, gleaming cutlery and glass, and in the centre of the table a Sèvres bowl containing a beautful arrangement of crimson roses, their perfume filling the room. Quiet classical music drifted down from speakers high in each corner, and across the two floor-to-ceiling windows were long, silver lace curtains, billowing gently in the breeze.

'This is beautiful!' Elspeth stood as if spellbound, by the door. 'Do you dine like this every night?' she asked, glancing up into Luke's face.

'We have done ever since I came,' interposed Colette, smiling. 'Isn't it romantic?'

Both Elspeth and Luke turned to stare at her. She assumed a cold proud countenance, aware that she was now challenging the pair of them. Elspeth seemed to feel it incumbent on her to answer, but all she said was,

'Very romantic.'

'Sit down, Jennifer—Elspeth.'

Luke was uncomfortable, decided Colette with some considerable satisfaction. She had not finished with him yet—not by any means! With nothing to lose she could carry this farce to any lengths she liked.

He sent her a glowering look as she sat down; she returned it with a lovely smile and saw the muscles round his mouth contract.

During the meal she fell silent, allowing Luke and Elspeth to talk. But soon it was borne in upon her that almost every word he uttered was a probe. He was asking about her life, and when she said that her father had died suddenly of a heart attack he spoke not one word of sympathy. Colette remembered the scene on that last night, when Lewis was so furious and Luke treated him with such cold contempt. And that was the night he said goodbye to Elspeth.

He was speaking now about Mrs Whitney and her daughter. Colette never raised her head from her plate as he said,

'When did they leave?'

'The day following that wedding you went to. Colette was there. . . .' Elspeth's voice trailed to silence and Colette glanced up. Elspeth's face was taut suddenly. She was recalling with some considerable embarrassment her words about his having told her he had had business to attend to. Obviously he hadn't intended to get her an invitation for the wedding.

'They left the day following?' Luke frowned, his fork half way to his mouth. 'Where did they go?' His voice was short and demanding, bringing a flash of angry enquiry to Elspeth's eyes.

'I wouldn't know,' she replied. 'Does it matter?'

'Your father would have turned Colette out that night if——'

'Luke—please,' broke in Elspeth. 'I couldn't help what my father did. . . .' She trailed off, flushing slightly, remembering that she herself had been in a virulent mood that night . . . and she was aware that Luke was remembering too.

'Did you ever hear what happened to them?' asked Luke persistently, his unfathomable gaze fixed on Colette's bent head.

'No. Colette had got herself a young man and they went off in his car—well, it might have been a hired car, I don't know. I wasn't in when they went, but Father was. They never even said goodbye to him—just got into the car, with their belongings, and drove away. That was the last we ever heard of them.'

A small silence followed, and Colette was forced to look up, forced by some compelling influence exerted by the man sitting opposite to her. His face was a mask, his black eyes fixed.

He said quietly, addressing Elspeth,

'Colette married the young man——'

'How do you know? I couldn't imagine anyone wanting to marry her. You said yourself that she was so badly disfigured that no one would want her. You laughed when I told you she had a crush on you....' She stopped slowly, halted by something in the atmosphere, and glanced from one to the other. Colette's eyes were meeting Luke's across the table, a sort of desolation not unmingled with reproach in hers, and in his a deep contrition ... and an apology.

The silence prevailed, with no one attempting to break it. Colette had known, a few seconds ago, that her act had come to an end, that Luke had guessed who she was. But even if enlightenment had not come to him it would have done so now, for she was quite unable to hide her feelings at hearing Elspeth's remark about Luke's laughing derision on being told that Colette had a crush on him. She drew her gaze from his at last, soft colour mantling her cheeks. Elspeth broke the silence, to ask if anything was wrong.

Luke said coolly, his eyes still on Colette, even

though she was intent now on her food, cutting herself
a piece of meat from one of the slices on her plate,

'The young man did marry Colette. He was wise; he
saw the beauty beneath the blemished surface ... saw
far more than you or I—or your father, Elspeth.
Colette's husband inherited a mansion and vast estate,
but was killed, along with her mother, in a car crash.
Colette was in the car too, but survived. Her injuries
were serious, though, and I have an idea that she nearly
died. However, she did not die; she had an operation
on her face——' He looked at her, his eyes all-examining. He saw her heightened colour, because of what he
had said about the beauty beneath the blemished surface, but was not interested in it at the moment as he
said, 'There must have been several operations, as this
miracle could not have been performed in one go.'

He stopped again, but neither girl spoke. Elspeth
was trying to articulate words but was unable to do so;
her expression was a mixture of incredulity and rejec-
tion. Obviously, thought Colette, she had not quite
worked it all out yet. 'She's a wealthy young lady today,' resumed Luke, 'having this huge estate. As she has
an efficient manager she decided to travel, and her
travels brought her here.' Another pause, and Colette,
marvelling at her own calm, and at the interest with
which she was listening to Luke's narrative, saw that
Elspeth had now grasped the whole story. Her mouth
had that ugly twist which had been so familiar to
Colette in those far-off days; her big eyes were dark and
cold as hoar frost.

'Colette met me when she came to Attikon,' Luke was
continuing, 'and decided to change her name——' He
looked at her and said, his tone changing dramatically,
taking on an inflection that brought disbelief to her
eyes but a surge of happiness to her heart, 'Tell me,

Colette, why did you change your name? I said Jennifer didn't suit you. And do you recall that night when you were tipsy, you actually asked me who Jennifer was? I knew then that there was some mystery....' He tailed off, watching her with a tender expression. He had been teasing her, and a lovely smile had broken through, although there were tears sparkling on her lashes. She was all confusion, scarcely able to accept that the miracle had happened, and that he loved her —oh, yes! There could be no mistaking that tone, and that expression. She had seen him tender before, when he was putting on an act, but this was different altogether ... it was the real thing.

She said absurdly, because no other words would come to her in this moment of wild, tumultuous joy,

'I wasn't tipsy—and it's most ungentlemanly of—of you to say so, Luke!'

He laughed and she caught her breath. For every hard line was erased, and even those onyx-black eyes were softened by the tenderest expression that had ever come to them.

'Darling, if I say you were tipsy, then you certainly were....' Something in her expression brought silence to his lips. He slid a glance to Elspeth, frowning at her. It dawned on Colette that he had forgotten she was there!

'She's—she's—Colette——' Elspeth's face had a greyish hue, her mouth was moving spasmodically as she stared, emotion causing her chest to heave. Warily Colette looked at her, for she knew from past experience that the woman's temper could rise to the point of hysteria. 'She can't be!' snarled Elspeth inconsistently. 'No operation could do this——'

'Plastic surgery did do it, Elspeth,' interrupted Colette in an effort to avoid a scene. 'I had several operations, over a period of eight months and this was the result.'

Black hatred looked out from Elspeth's eyes; she was losing dignity and control, as she had done on that night when Luke had brought Colette back from the wedding.

'It isn't true! Something's wrong—— And all that backchat between you just now—what was it all about? I suppose you're his tart, his——'

'That'll do!' Luke, his face like thunder, his tone causing even Colette to tremble, rose from his chair. 'You're talking about the girl I'm going to marry!' He clapped his hands for Davos, who came on the instant, having been just outside the door, waiting for the summons that would tell him the course was finished and the next one could be served. Elspeth, unheeding of his entry into the room, pointed a trembling, accusing finger at Colette.

'You—you asked me here only to humiliate me! I hate you—*hate* you. . . .' Her voice dropped to a whisper as she added, 'He'll never marry you—you poor fool!' She appeared to be choked by the strength of her emotions, but she seemed on the point of continuing for all that. Luke was before her, saying quietly to Davos,

'Have someone drive Miss Whitney to her hotel. She's not very well.'

'Thanks!' Elspeth flung her serviette on to her dinner plate. 'I can get back without your help!' And, quivering with rage, she flounced from the room, slamming the door behind her.

'Mr Lucius——' began Davos, bewildered. 'What——?'

'Leave us,' ordered Luke. 'I shall ring when I want

you to serve the next course. Oh, and give Miss Whitney her wrap.'

It was to be a long time before he rang. Colette, safe in his embrace, looked adoringly into her lover's eyes.

'Is it true—really true?'

'Dearest, how many more times must I say it?'

'It's just that I can't believe it, that's all.'

They had been talking since Elspeth left, and many things had been cleared up. Luke admitted that he had not been at all enamoured with giving up his freedom, but he also admitted that he had begun to accept that his bachelor days were coming to an end.

'You affected me as no other woman had ever done before—right from the moment I saw you, in the light from the launch and the lights from the shore. I was drawn to you, but there was always something mysterious, something about you I couldn't understand. You had a secret, that was obvious, since you refused to talk about your early life. I felt I'd met you before, but the impression passed each time it came, simply because I've a very good memory for faces——' He paused to take her face in his hand and stare into it, then to bend his head and kiss her quivering lips. And then he continued, 'I had never seen this lovely face before, and that was what caused me so much trouble and frustration. Your voice ... illusive threads of memory. And then last evening when Elspeth stared at your hair....' He shook his head. 'You never answered me when I asked why you changed your name?'

'It was—was——' She broke off shyly. He tilted her face with a gentle finger under her chin.

'That "crush", sweet ... it was love?' A statement, though posed as a question, and Colette nodded her head. 'So, with a new face and an entirely new name, you were hoping. . . .' It was Luke's turn to break off and Colette's turn to finish for him,

'. . . to make you love me, Luke. I felt that if you knew who I was, you wouldn't want me. If I could make you fall in love with me first, then of course I would have to tell you everything, I said to myself.'

'Dearest, you make me feel a brute—I *was* a brute! To think I could callously deceive you, cajole you into coming back here—I don't deserve that you should love me, Colette. I meant nothing good by you even though, at the back of my mind, I wanted more than a lover; I knew that I wanted a friend, a companion——' He shook his head as if exasperated with himself. 'I wanted, my precious, a wife.'

'But—but if you had had me as a—a pillow-friend you'd never have married me, would you?'

He nodded, and his face was serious and tender and very wise, all at the same time.

'Yes, I would, Colette. When a man meets his last love there is nothing for him but to make her his own, no matter what might have gone before. Yes, my precious darling, you and I would have been married even if we'd been lovers first.'

Although looking into his eyes she could not doubt his words, she was glad they had not been lovers first. She saw his tender smile and lifted her face, inviting his kiss. He laughed softly, and for the next few passionate moments she was swept into the realm of sheer ecstasy by the tender savagery of his lovemaking. And even when he stopped kissing her he held her close to him, caressing her slender body with his own. He would be a passionate lover, she thought, a masterful conqueror to whom she would be glad to surrender. She thought momentarily of home, and mentioned to him that she ought to sell up.

They would talk about it later, he promised, saying that she must not do anything impulsively. She had previously told him about Philip, and Luke said that she might prefer to leave the estate in his care.

And, thinking of home, she quite naturally thought of the secret drawer, and the faded rose that lay within it. Some day she would tell him about it—but not yet. It was still her secret, reminder of a pretence, and of a love she never dared to hope would be reciprocated.

She was his last love. He had said the words she had cherished in her dream world but had never thought to hear uttered by the man she loved. Her eyes became misted over and she felt foolish and tried to hide her face by burying it in his jacket. Sensitive to her emotion, Luke tilted her chin, his hand warm and tender and caressing. But his eyes widened as he saw the tears.

'Beloved, my dearest—why are you crying?'

At the tender anxiety in his voice the tears began to fall on to her cheeks.

'It's really n-nothing to—to cry a-about,' she told him on a little choking sob. 'You see, I—always wanted to b-be your last love—and you've said it—just now. . . .' Her voice trailed to a sheepish silence as she noticed the smile of tender amusement that had come to his lips.

'You idiot,' he chided softly, bringing out a handkerchief to dry her face. 'Crying——' He shook his head. 'You adorable little idiot! Shall I beat you or kiss you?'

'I'd much rather you kissed me, Luke,' she told him, managing a shaky little laugh.

'Nothing,' he murmured softly, 'would give me greater pleasure.' And, bending his head, he suited action to his words.

Harlequin Plus
A WORD ABOUT THE AUTHOR

Anne Hampson, one of Harlequin's most prolific writers, is the author of more than thirty Romances and thirty Presents. She holds the distinction of having written the first two Harlequin Presents, in 1973: *Gates of Steel* and *Master of Moonrock*.

Anne is also one of Harlequin's most widely traveled authors, her research taking her to ever new and exotic settings. And wherever she goes she takes copious notes, absorbs all she can about the flora and fauna and becomes completely involved with the people and their customs.

Anne taught school for four years before turning to writing full-time. Her outside interests include collecting antiques, rocks and fossils, and travel is one of her greatest pleasures—but only by ship; like many, she's afraid of flying.

What does she like most? "Sparkling streams, clear starry nights, the breeze on my face. Anything, in fact, that has to do with nature."